SCARLETT

A CREEPY HOLLOW STORY

Also by Rachel Morgan

THE CREEPY HOLLOW SERIES

The Faerie Guardian

The Faerie Prince

The Faerie War

A Faerie's Secret

A Faerie's Revenge

A Faerie's Curse

Glass Faerie

Shadow Faerie

Rebel Faerie

CREEPY HOLLOW
COMPANION STORIES

Scarlett

Raven

SCARLETT

A CREEPY HOLLOW STORY

RACHEL MORGAN

RACHEL
MORGAN

This story takes place several months before
The Faerie Guardian (Creepy Hollow, Book One).

CHAPTER ONE

SHE WORE A RED DRESS THAT NIGHT. NOT CARNELIAN RED or wine red, but bright, brilliant red. Red that stood out in a crowd. Scarlet red. It wrapped snugly around her frame, accentuating her narrow waist, binding her legs together, and somehow producing a not-insignificant amount of cleavage from her normally barely there chest.

Beth had never worn anything like it.

The money she saved from hours of scooping ice cream at Peppa's Parlor after school normally went toward far more ordinary things. Miniature plants for her bedroom, school-appropriate clothing, and topping up the grocery bill—since Dad never gave her enough money when he sent her to the store every week. But tonight was a special occasion, and it warranted a special dress. A special dress she hoped Dad wouldn't force her to change out of.

She couldn't decide whether he'd hate this dress or not. She knew he *should* hate it—should hate seeing his sixteen-year-old daughter wearing something so provocative—but it was more likely he wouldn't care enough to have an opinion. He'd never seen his daughter as much more than a burdensome consequence of his accidental wanderings into a realm beyond his own.

Beth styled her long, dark hair into voluminous curls, which she pinned back on one side and allowed to cascade over her other shoulder. She angled the wardrobe door and admired the effect in the tiny mirror stuck inside.

A whistle broke the silence, and Beth threw a glance over her shoulder at the window. Barely an arm's length away, Zoe leaned on her own cracked, chipped window ledge. "Hot date tonight?" she asked with a grin. Haphazardly placed, like a child's building blocks tossed together in too small a space, the rundown houses on Miller Lane afforded their occupants little privacy. Good thing Beth and Zoe had been friends ever since Zoe moved in five years ago, poked her raven-black head into the space between their two houses, and complimented Beth on her miniature plant collection.

"Don't pretend you know nothing about it," Beth said, returning Zoe's smile. "And I told you I'd be making a special effort for tonight. I only get a one-year anniversary once."

"Well Jack is *definitely* going to notice your special effort, no doubt about that."

Beth ducked her head as a blush heated her face. She'd always thought of herself as rather plain. The shy girl with brown hair and brown eyes. She'd inherited barely a shred of her mother's stunning beauty. But tonight, wearing this dress, she felt different. Tonight she wouldn't be that plain girl.

"Where's he taking you?" Zoe asked as she picked at the flaking paint on her window ledge.

Beth frowned. "I thought you'd know already."

Zoe pasted an innocent look onto her face, but Beth stared her down. "Okay, fine," Zoe said, slumping against the window frame. "I know everything. It's totally boring, and you'll totally love it, and it's a complete waste of that gorgeous dress because *no one* else is going to see it."

Beth smiled. "Sounds perfect."

"I can't give away anything more."

"You shouldn't have given away *anything*," Beth chided her. "But I won't tell Jack."

"Thanks. He's been known to hurt me for giving his secrets away."

"I know." Beth laughed as the memory of Jack chasing his sister around their tiny backyard with a pillow came to mind. "I'm surprised he tells you anything anymore."

"He doesn't. But, you know, sharing a house means I can't help accidentally discovering things."

"Oh, yes, I'm sure it's accidental." Beth reached for the silver chain hanging from the wardrobe doorknob. She fastened the clasp behind her neck and looked into the mirror again. Delicate silver letters spelling the word *Beth* lay against her chest just below her throat. Lastly, she picked up an ornate silver ring with a large pearl sitting atop it—the one and only thing her mother had ever given her—and pushed it onto her left forefinger. "Okay. I think I'm ready."

"You know that necklace is a bit too, uh, childish for that dress, right?"

"I know, but Jack gave it to me, and I love it."

"Yeah, yeah." Zoe sighed, then added, "Don't forget lipstick."

"Oh, lipstick, right." Beth turned back to her wardrobe, but stopped. "Darn, I completely forgot to get a color that matches the dress." Makeup had never been high on her priority list, and after purchasing the dress itself and checking that the simple black heels she kept aside for special occasions looked okay with the dress, she'd thought the outfit complete.

"I've probably got something that'll work." Zoe disappeared from sight and Beth heard her rummaging through the contents of one of her drawers. "Got it. This should be close enough." She reappeared and tossed a small tube to Beth.

Beth caught it easily, pulled the lid off, and stepped in front of her mirror once more. She applied the bright red color, pressed her lips together, and turned back to the window to give Zoe the most seductive pout she could summon without giggling.

Zoe mimed fainting against the window frame before fanning herself. "Look at you, you sexy siren."

Beth froze. The lipstick slipped from her fingers. "I'm not—I'm not a—"

Siren.

Why would Zoe say that? She couldn't possibly *know*, could she? No. Zoe had no idea how true her words were. No idea of the world hiding just beyond her sight.

"You okay?" Zoe asked, watching Beth closely.

"Yes, just being clumsy." Beth dismissed the moment with a laugh she hoped sounded natural as she bent down—with great difficulty, given the tightness of the dress—and retrieved the lipstick.

"I was joking, Beth," Zoe said as Beth straightened. "We all know you're not a temptress. I seriously don't expect you to seduce my brother and then ... I don't know, *eat* him or whatever."

"That's not—" *That's not how it works*, she wanted to say, but stopped herself. "That's so gross, Zoe," she said, adding in another laugh.

"I know." Zoe shuddered. "I should *not* be using the words 'seduce' and 'brother' in the same sentence."

"I was referring to the eating part."

"Oh, yeah, that too." A bang sounded from the direction of Zoe's front porch. She looked over her shoulder, then said, "I think Jack just left."

A nervous shiver ran down Beth's spine. "Are you sure I look okay?" She cast a final glance down at herself—and felt odd all of a sudden, as if her limbs and head were buzzing. It was a strange sort of dizziness. She'd felt it before, but it was starting to happen more often. She should probably visit a doctor. The moment passed and she looked up once more. Through the window, Zoe stared at her with a frown. "What?" Beth asked. "Did I smudge my makeup?"

"No." Zoe shook her head. "You just ... look really beautiful, that's all."

Beth blew a kiss across the open space to her best friend. "Thanks, Zo."

She grabbed her purse and hurried downstairs as quickly as her heels allowed. Dad was slumped in his favorite chair in front of the TV. Based on the continuous stream of commentary overlaying a dull roar of cheering and shouting, Beth guessed he was watching some form of sport. She didn't look closely enough to see which one. Instead, she kept her gaze focused on the front door as she walked past the living room.

"Where are you going?" Dad called as she passed the door. "And what—" He sat up straighter as she leaned into the doorway to look at him. In a low voice, he asked, "What is that?"

She knew what he was referring to. "It's a dress," she said, moving fully into the doorway and injecting her voice with as much confidence as she could muster. "And I'm going on a date with Jack."

Instead of telling her to go back upstairs and change, Dad simply stared, his eyes narrowing and his jaw clenching tightly. Beth placed a hand on her hip and stared defiantly back at him. For once in her life, she wouldn't back down. For once, she wouldn't feel guilty simply for existing.

And then—that odd feeling of dizzy power vibrated through her once more, followed abruptly by a shock that zapped her arm like static electricity on a dry day.

Ding dong.

The shock was gone, and so was the vibration, and all Beth heard were two growled words leaving her father's lips: "Get. Out."

CHAPTER TWO

BETH HAD ALWAYS KNOWN HER FATHER DIDN'T CARE much for her. She'd listened to her classmates whining about the anger and disappointment of their parents if any of them broke the rules at home, and she'd envied them, believing that nothing could be worse than a parent who didn't care at all. But tonight she'd discovered something worse.

It was worse to know that her father hated her.

She pushed aside the ache in her heart and rushed to the front door. She pulled it open—and there stood Jack, dressed in his smartest jacket, his dark hair buzzed short just the way it suited him, and his warm eyes smiling at her. Those eyes widened as he took her in. "You look … incredible."

With her throat still too tight for her to utter a single word, she simply melted against him. His arms wrapped around her, secure and comforting. And just like that, her world was right again.

"Hey, what's wrong?" he asked.

"Let's go." She reached back and pulled the door shut. Jack took her hand as they walked down the front steps. High above them, purple-black clouds blotted out the evening sky. Beth probably should have brought a coat, but there was no way she was going back inside now. They reached Jack's car—more a patchwork collection of rusted pieces of metal than an actual vehicle—and he held the passenger door open for her. She didn't speak as they began driving, but Jack kept his hand resting on her knee, and that was enough to ease the pain of that moment inside the house. By the time Jack pulled up near the lake, Dad's last words to her had receded to the far reaches of her memory, and the nervous excitement she'd felt while getting dressed coursed once more through her body. She'd been to the lake before, of course. She loved it here.

The water calls to us ...

Unbidden, the distant memory of her mother's words rose to the surface of her mind. She dismissed them as she climbed from the car. As much as she might wish it in the secret depths of her heart, she was nothing like her mother. It wasn't only water and the untamed power of the ocean that she loved. Being anywhere outside made her happy. Fields, forests, mountains. Not that she often had the opportunity to spend time in nature. The dull and nearly dead town of Holtyn saw to that. But Jack had taken her hiking several times, driving hours and hours in search of hills and mountains, and they'd even visited the beach twice this past summer. The rest of the time, Beth made do with the lake on the outskirts of town.

Jack had parked on the overgrown side, though. The side no one ever came to because too many tangled plants blocked the way to the water. She didn't question him, though. He came around to her side of the car and took her hand. "You might have a little bit of trouble with those shoes, but I promise I won't let you trip." Then he led her, not away from the overgrown tangle of bushes and trees, but toward it. He pulled back one of the larger branches so she could duck beneath it. She saw then that a path had been cleared.

"Did you do this?" she asked, looking back at him through the lattice of leaves and twigs.

"Remember I said I was busy last week?"

"Yes. I didn't see you the whole weekend."

He stooped beneath the branch before letting it fall back into place behind him. He beamed at her. "Now you know where I was. Keep going," he added, urging her forward.

Beth continued along the newly formed path, being careful to avoid the sharp edges where Jack must have hacked his way through the branches just days ago. After several more careful steps, she came to a clearing right beside the water. A picnic blanket lay upon the uneven grass, with a basket beside it and jars of candles all around. "This is that spot," she said in amazement, looking out across the water to the opposite shore. "That spot we always see from the other side but have never been able to get to."

"Yes," Jack said. "Happy first anniversary." As emotion tightened Beth's throat, making it difficult to speak, he hastily added, "It's not a fancy restaurant or anything, but I know you love the lake, and you've always wished you could find a way to this side, so I figured—"

"It's amazing. I couldn't have asked for anything better." She had often wished she could run away and live in that other world, the world she'd been born for. But then she'd fallen in love with the boy next door, and now moments like this reminded her that she didn't need that other world after all. This one was enough for her.

"It's just a little bit magical, isn't it?" Jack said, reaching for her hand.

"Yes." Not the kind of magical she knew of, but as close to magical as anything could be in this world.

They sat on the blanket and Beth kicked her shoes off while Jack switched his phone to silent and left it by the picnic basket. Still feeling a little nervous, Beth began describing the miniature terrarium she'd constructed that morning inside a hanging teardrop vase. Jack listened as he poured a drink for each of them. Sparkling grape juice, icy enough to send a shiver down her arms as she took a sip. "I'm sorry, I didn't expect it to be this cold tonight," Jack said, removing his jacket and placing it around Beth's shoulders.

"It's okay. I have you to keep me warm." She put her cup down so she could push her arms into the sleeves of the jacket. If she'd been dressed like this when she left the house, Dad might not have been so furious. He might not have looked at her with such hatred. She pressed her lips together as she realized the cracks his words had caused in her heart were still there.

Jack ran his fingers delicately through her hair and asked, "Do you want to tell me what's wrong?"

She looked up, surprised. She had meant to hide her sadness, but clearly she wasn't doing a very good job. "No, not now. I don't want to ruin tonight."

"But if something's bothering you, then rather get it out. That way it won't bother you anymore, and the night won't be ruined."

She looked down at the blanket. "My dad ..." Jack nodded, as if he'd known it was something to do with Dad. Of course he knew. Whenever something was wrong, it was almost always to do with the nonexistent relationship between Beth and her father. "It's just something he said before I left. He ... I've always believed I mean nothing to him—"

"Don't say that."

"—but I was wrong. I mean *less* than nothing to him."

"It doesn't matter," Jack said, and Beth was grateful he didn't try to contradict her. Didn't try to convince her that her father did, in fact, care. He knew it wasn't true just as much as she did. Instead, he leaned forward and pressed a gentle kiss against her cheek. "You mean everything to me, my beautiful scarlet lady," he whispered into her ear.

"Scarlett," she whispered back, tasting the name on her tongue. "I like that. It sounds so exotic."

"It does." He kissed her earlobe, then pulled back slightly. With one finger, he touched the silver name resting beneath her throat. "But I'm not sure it entirely fits the sweet girl I know you are inside."

"Maybe I don't want to be that sweet girl all the time," she said, looking up at him between lashes painted dark with mascara. "Maybe tonight I want to be Scarlett."

Scarlett ... The name made her feel stronger, braver. It made her feel more like someone her mother would be pleased with instead of the entirely ordinary girl she had turned out to be. It made her feel like she could almost, possibly ... be one of *them*.

"Scarlett," Jack whispered, a fire igniting in his eyes as she held his gaze, daring him to see her as more than the sweet girl next door.

And then the corners of his lips turned up, and she found a giggle escaping her lips just as Jack's face crumpled with amusement. They fell against each other, their laughter mingling together, and it seemed to Beth that the cracks in her heart were almost healed. As their laughter subsided, she found herself on her back on the blanket with Jack leaning over her, his smiling face close to hers. He kissed her neck, his fingers slid between hers, and when he looked at her again, his gaze was almost adoring. "It doesn't matter what name I call you," he said. "I'll always love you."

A shiver raced across her skin, and at first she thought it was because of Jack's words and the way he was looking at her. But then she realized the strange feeling had returned. The vibration that hummed throughout her body, making her feel light and heavy at the same time. She wanted to make a mental note to stop putting it off and phone the doctor the next day, but there wasn't a single thought she could hold onto with Jack looking at her like that.

As if nothing else existed in the world but her.

"You are more beautiful tonight than you've ever been before," he whispered.

His lips found hers, and she pulled him closer. Her eyes slid closed. She forgot everything—Dad's angry words, the picnic blanket beneath her, the soft patter of rain that had begun to fall. All that mattered was Jack's body pressed against hers, his fingers sliding into her hair, his breaths becoming shallow as their kiss deepened. She dug her fingers into his back, feeling the muscles beneath his shirt, imagining his strength.

As if with a great effort, Jack pulled his lips from hers and took a deep breath. Opening her eyes a fraction, she jokingly said, "Is this where you tell me I'm taking your breath away?"

"I feel … I can't …" He pulled away from her embrace and clutched his chest.

Alarmed, Beth sat up. "What's wrong?"

"I …"

"Jack?"

He tried to speak, but his shallow breaths had become gasps. He shook his head and clutched more desperately at his chest. He collapsed onto his side on the blanket. With icy fear shooting through her, Beth scrambled across the blanket and grabbed Jack's phone. She tapped the numbers with shaking fingers before returning to his side. "Breathe, okay? Just breathe."

They were the most useless words she'd ever uttered.

She saw the terror in his eyes as his horrible, rasping gasps became slower and slower. She wrapped her hand around his and squeezed it tight. His back arched, and he let out a terrible moaning gasp as a surge of power rushed through Beth's body.

Shocked, frozen in place, her eyes moved to their clasped hands. Realization, slow and terrible and inevitable, coalesced into a single impossible thought.

Siren.

She snatched her hand away from Jack's and dropped the phone. "No," she whispered. "No, no, no."

"… your emergency?" came the disembodied voice from the phone. "Hello?"

Jack's eyelids fluttered weakly. His chest barely rose and fell. Biting down on her shaking lip, Beth picked up the phone. She forced herself to speak, but her voice sounded far away as she named the lake and the area before dropping the phone as if it burned.

"I'm sorry," she whispered, inching slowly away from Jack. "I'm sorry, I'm sorry, I'm sorry."

Then she pushed herself to her feet and ran. Twigs slapped her arms and rain wet her face as she tore along the makeshift path. She cried out as the sharp edge of a branch sliced across her leg, but she didn't stop running. She kept going until she pushed past the final branch and stumbled out beside Jack's car. She reached for the door—but where could she go? Not home. Dad would cast her out if she'd truly become the thing he hated most. She had to leave—she couldn't go near anyone she cared about ever again—but the thought of being on her own terrified her. How would she survive?

And Jack.

Jack.

"What have I done?" she whispered to the night.

The wailing cry of an ambulance reached her ears. It wasn't

far off. Of course it wasn't. Nothing ever happened in Holtyn. This was probably the first emergency all week.

Beth looked down at her shaking hands. She stared at the ring. It was the only option left to her now. She gripped the pearl between her thumb and forefinger. She twisted it around three times.

And the world vanished.

CHAPTER THREE

A WHIRLWIND OF COLOR SPUN BETH AROUND AND AROUND before dumping her onto a beach of warm sand where she stumbled and fell to her knees. She stayed there, digging her fingers into the fine white sand, catching her breath, and feeling the magic-infused air drift across her skin. Though a decade had passed since she'd last been here, she knew this was the right place. That almost imperceptible hum that existed in the sand, the water, even the air, was the same hum that now pulsed through her own body. A hum she had never noticed until she'd been sent to live in a world devoid of it.

Beth clenched her fingers, watching a ripple of blue light dance through the sand away from her hands and vanish as it reached the water. She scooped the sand up and let it sift between her fingers. As the grains hit the ground, they became

crystals. White crystals that scattered around her knees, sparkling in the afternoon light before disintegrating into sand once
more. She stood and looked out across the water. The rays of
the setting sun glittered like fiery orange gems upon the ocean's
surface, far beyond the breaking waves where white foam
became galloping horses that tumbled and vanished as they
reached the shore. This world was alive in a way that the other
world—her father's world—could never be. And it was just as
glorious in reality as it was in her dreams.

But Jack …

She squeezed her eyes shut as guilt tightened like a fist
around her heart. He would be fine, wouldn't he? She hadn't
drawn much power from his body. She hadn't even known she
was doing it. And the ambulance was almost at the lake when
she left. Jack would be fine, she told herself. But she couldn't
go back until she was certain she'd never hurt him again. She
opened her eyes and turned around—

And there stood her mother, Evaline. Dazzling, fearsome,
perfectly graceful.

"Bessie?" Evaline said, and the terrified girl had to remind
herself that she was only five and a half the last time her
mother saw her. That was the age at which Evaline sent Beth to
live with her father. It was clear by then that she possessed no
magic, and Evaline had no use for a daughter who was
essentially human. "Bessie," her mother repeated, the questioning tone gone from her voice.

Bessie. Beth had come to hate that name early on. After a
week of being called Bessie the Cow by her new human classmates, she'd informed her father, her teacher, and the other

children—in an uncharacteristic show of confidence—that they had made a mistake; her name was not Bessie but Beth. That confidence was nowhere to be found now, so instead of answering, Beth merely nodded.

"You look awful," Evaline said. Beth looked down at the oversized jacket and the torn dress. Dirt smudged her feet and hands. She noticed, however, that her legs bore no scratches, and above the smeared dribble of blood where there should have been an open wound, only a narrow cut marred her skin. "Beneath all that mess, however," Evaline added, "you seem to have turned out rather lovely. Almost lovely enough to be one of us." She folded her arms over her chest. "What are you doing here? I told you there was only one reason you should ever return. I hope you haven't forgotten that."

A spark of annoyance ignited Beth's terrified core, heating her chest and running down to her fingertips. This was her mother. Her own *mother*. Couldn't she at least pretend to be glad to see her daughter after all these years? Finally finding her voice, she said, "I haven't forgotten. That's why I'm here."

Her mother tilted her head to the side, her gaze narrowing slightly. She looked around, seeming to search for something, before her gaze snapped back to Beth. "Is that *you* I'm sensing?"

Beth hated the look of shock on Evaline's face, as if it were so impossible that her disappointment of a daughter might have turned out magical after all. She raised her chin, attempting to portray the self-assurance she wished she felt. "I—I think so. I've been feeling different lately, and then tonight I was ... I was with someone, and when I touched him,

18

it felt as though ... I'd sucked the energy out of his body and into mine."

Evaline took a few steps toward Beth—though 'step' was a loose term; she seemed to glide more than walk—as an expression of wonder came over her face. "You're one of us after all. You truly are my daughter."

A hesitant smile tugged the edges of Beth's lips as the tension eased from her chest. She'd been waiting her whole life to hear those words.

But Jack ...

An ache pulsed through her chest. "Will he be okay? The boy I was with. Will he recover?"

Evaline tilted her head. "Did you take all his life force?"

"No, not even close. I mean, I don't think so. We weren't in contact for long after it started happening."

Evaline's tone was dismissive as she said, "I'm sure he'll be fine then." She moved closer and wrapped her arms briefly around Beth. It was barely a hug, just enough for Beth to feel Evaline's hands press lightly against her back, and her sleek, ebony hair tickle her cheek. But it was the most affection Beth could remember her mother ever showing her.

"Come," Evaline said. "Let's go home."

* * *

Beth remembered the rocks that led to the sirens' home. She remembered standing atop them, staring out at the wild waters, wishing in her young heart that she could be everything her mother wanted her to be. Evaline traversed the rocks with practiced ease, while Beth trailed several steps behind her, slipping and stumbling and grasping onto the rocks. Wherever she placed her hand, the rough, weathered surface lit up, a different color each time, and she wondered if the rocks were now enchanted that way or if it was her magic creating the light.

The rocks hid a shallow pool that lapped upon the shores of a concealed beach. Beyond that, more rocks rose sharply, jutting out at odd angles and concealing the entrance to the sirens' home. Evaline led Beth around the pool, beneath the archway carved into the stone, through a short tunnel, and then—

Beth was finally home. It was familiar and strange and beautiful all at once. Ahead of her was the vast oval-shaped garden she remembered playing in as a child. Fountains, pools, statues and hedges created the perfect setting for a game of hide-and-seek. An open corridor of white marble, held up by pillars carved with exquisite detail, encircled the oval space. On the outer edge of the corridor, archways of greenery led to individual gardens and homes.

It was toward one of these archways that Evaline was no doubt leading her. Whichever one was now her home. A young girl ran across their path, then stopped to lean against a pillar and stare at Beth. Beth looked away, feeling self-conscious in her oversized jacket and blood-smudged legs. She clasped her hands together and felt sand on her palms. Although, sand didn't feel quite like that, did it? Surprise jolted through her as she looked down and found glitter falling between her fingers.

She lifted one arm and watched the glitter trail through the air behind her.

"Bessie, dear, please try to control yourself," Evaline said. "You're radiating magic everywhere."

"It's Beth."

Evaline stopped abruptly, causing Beth to almost walk into her. She looked over her shoulder. "Excuse me?"

Swallowing her unease, Beth said, "My name is Beth, not Bessie."

Evaline's gaze shifted to the silver pendant resting at the base of Beth's neck. Her eyes, bright and dangerous and unforgiving, moved back up to meet Beth's. "Beth, *dear*," she repeated, "control yourself. You're radiating magic everywhere."

Everywhere ... Beth thought back to the light glowing within the rocks, the sand turning to crystals, and the galloping sea foam horses. Were those all products of the magic she had no control over?

"Bessie? Is that you?"

Beth looked behind her. A girl with long, shimmering copper locks stood between two pillars, watching her. A memory of two little girls running along the beach, their bare feet kicking sand into the air behind them, rose to the front of Beth's mind. "Delphine?" she asked.

"Hurry up, Beth," Evaline said, her voice tugging Beth back to the present. "You'll have time for old friends later."

She continued along the corridor, Beth hurrying behind her, and turned beneath the archway at the far end of the oval. The archway that was larger and prettier than all the others.

"Wait," Beth said, her footsteps slowing. "Is this ... do you live here now?"

Evaline laughed. "No, I am not Ruler. I have advanced to Second, though, so who knows what might happen one day."

"But—I—should I not clean up before meeting with the Ruler?"

"I'm well aware that you're not properly dressed, but newcomers are required to report to the Ruler's residence immediately upon entering our community." She tugged the jacket off Beth, then waved her hand near Beth's legs and hands until the dirt and blood disappeared. "There. You look a little more acceptable now." Evaline turned to face the Ruler's residence, which was covered in leafy green vines. "Don't dawdle, Beth. Our Ruler doesn't like to be kept waiting."

* * *

Beth's meeting with the Ruler, a woman named Lillian who was guarded by spear-wielding women and who seemed vaguely familiar, was brief. Lillian walked around her as Evaline spoke. She sniffed at the air, touched Beth's rain-dampened hair, and then congratulated Evaline on the return of her daughter. It was odd and creepy, and Beth hardly breathed until she was out of the house.

"She wasn't Ruler when I was a child," Beth said when they reached the corridor.

"No. She was elected three years ago." Other than that, Evaline offered no further explanation.

There were more women about now. Young and old, all of

them beautiful, and all of them watching her. No men, of course. Siren men lived separately. They were necessary for continuing the siren race, but energy and power could not be drawn from them, which meant they were otherwise useless to siren women.

Evaline turned beneath another archway, and when they entered the small house, she said, "Welcome home, my daughter." She led Beth into the sitting room, which was just as white and bright as the marble outside. "I have only one bedroom, so you'll need to sleep in here until we can convert my study into a room for you. Or add on a separate room." She tapped her chin. "Yes, that would be better. Oh, don't sit on that until you've had a bath," she added quickly as Beth hovered near the spotless white chaise longue. "Come, the bathing pool is this way."

As Beth soaked in a pool of steaming water, her mother sat on the stool beside the tall mirror in the corner of the room and brushed her lustrous hair. "We have much to do," she said. "You'll need to learn more about control, and there are plenty of other lessons to catch up on. History and politics and the like. And, of course, we should have a celebration. A party to welcome you home."

To someone like Beth who'd never been comfortable as the center of attention, that sounded like an awful idea. "Uh, okay," she said as she moved to the edge of the pool. "Does it take long to learn control?"

"It can take several months for a child, but since you're much older, I hope you'll find control easier to grasp. Then again—" she lowered her brush "—nothing about your magical development has been normal, so I can't say how long it will take you to achieve control."

Beth nodded, trying not to feel daunted by everything she still had to learn. "It felt as though my magic appeared out of nowhere, but now that I think about, I remember strange things happening sometimes when I was younger." She took a breath before continuing, telling herself that this was her mother and that she shouldn't be afraid to speak more than a few words to her. "I fought with Dad once. I was angrier than I'd ever been, and even though I was scared of shouting at him, I couldn't help it. I screamed all my anger out and then ran upstairs. When I got to my bedroom, I found that all my books and papers had blown off my desk and scattered onto the floor. The window was open, and I told myself it must have been a particularly strong gust of wind, but I remember thinking how strange it was because it hadn't been windy at all that day."

"Mm hmm," Evaline murmured. She was once again brushing her hair, and Beth couldn't tell if she was listening or not. She decided to continue anyway.

"Another time at school, a friend passed me a joke on a piece of paper. It was so funny, but I wasn't supposed to laugh because we were in the middle of a lesson, so I did my absolute best to hold my giggles in. That's when the tap in the basin at the back of the classroom popped off and sprayed water everywhere. The teacher thought it was a plumbing issue, but maybe it was me. There were other strange things that happened, but I never put them all together and thought of myself as the cause of any of them. Not until … now."

"I see," Evaline said, sounding almost bored.

Beth climbed out of the pool and reached for the white robe Evaline had hung behind the door for her. She pulled it on and asked, "Do you think all those incidents were caused by my magic trying to get out?"

"Possibly." Evaline stood and examined her appearance in the mirror. "Interesting that your father didn't notice any of this."

"Yeah," Beth said quietly, but she knew why. Her father didn't notice much when it came to her. Well, except for when she'd come downstairs in the red dress. He'd taken notice then. And now, as she caught a glimpse of both her mother and herself in the mirror, she suddenly understood why. Her father had looked at her and seen Evaline—and he'd hated her for it.

CHAPTER FOUR

IT WAS INTIMIDATING AS HELL STANDING BEFORE A CROWD of stunningly beautiful women. Beth knew their intense beauty was only part of their siren magic, but the thought did nothing to lessen her insecurity. She wondered if her sudden awakening of magic had affected her own appearance. Once she'd cleaned up, her mother had commented on how enchantingly lovely she looked—possibly the nicest thing Evaline had ever said to her—but when Beth looked in the mirror, she couldn't see any difference. The difference, if there was one, must be a kind of glamour, visible only to others and not to herself.

As her tentative steps took her out from beneath the stone archway and onto the sand near the shimmering pool, Beth reminded herself that she belonged here now. She'd chosen a dress far less revealing than the one she'd worn to her disastrous date with Jack. The blue skirt was long and flowing, tickling her bare feet and skimming the sand behind her. The sleeves were a modest length, ending just above her elbows, but the neckline plunged a little more than she was comfortable with. It was one thing to bare her cleavage to the guy she loved, and quite another to put it on display before a group of women with assets far more enticing than her own. Feeling almost naked, she wrapped her arms around herself and waited.

Conversation stilled and every eye turned to her. She forced herself to look away from the examining gazes, focusing instead on the glittering rocks, the tiny lights floating in the air, and the music emanating faintly from somewhere behind her. Evaline, who had walked out of the tunnel at Beth's side, lifted her hand and laid it lightly on Beth's lower back as she began speaking. In tones as mesmerizing as any master storyteller's, she presented Beth to the siren community, spinning a heartwarming tale of homecoming and reunion. Beth noted that her previous lack of magic and forced exile from the community at an early age were never mentioned.

Evaline finished her story by encouraging everyone to make Beth feel welcome. The chattering started up once more, the music grew louder, and Beth felt her mother's hand pressing against her back, urging her forward. She took a few hesitant steps, trying not to meet anyone's gaze. She knew people were still looking at her. Still talking about her. Was she meant to approach someone and just begin a conversation? Or wait for someone to walk up to her?

This was awful. It was worse than the first day at a new school.

She was contemplating hiding behind a rock when she noticed someone coming toward her. Delphine, moving with gliding grace, her glorious copper curls tumbling over her shoulders. She greeted Beth with a grin. "I can't believe you're back." She leaned in as if for a hug, but, perhaps noticing the way Beth's arms tightened self-consciously around her chest, Delphine opted to rest her hand on Beth's upper arm instead, squeezing lightly before letting go. "I'm so happy you turned out to be magical after all. I was completely devastated after your mother sent you away. I cried myself to sleep every night for weeks."

Beth allowed herself to relax into a smile. "I'm willing to bet I cried a whole lot more than you did."

"Oh no, it must have been terrible! I've never even been into the human realm. Is it as boring as they say it is?"

Beth shrugged. "It has its perks." *Like Jack ...*

"Well, anyway." Delphine swung her arms at her sides. "Isn't it pretty out here tonight? We don't often have gatherings that involve the entire community."

"It is lovely," Beth said, wanting to smack herself over the head for not being able to come up with anything more intelligent to say.

"Do you remember how we used to sneak out here and watch the older girls training?" Delphine said, nodding toward the rocks on the other side of the pool. "I always thought it was so silly we had to practice the traditional arts, singing from the rocks to call the sailors. Don't we have better ways to draw men in these days?"

Beth chuckled. "Don't let my mother hear you say that. I've

been back little more than a day and I've already heard her practicing her singing."

Delphine rolled her eyes. "*Your* mother? I shouldn't let *my* mother hear me say things like that. She'd remind me how inappropriate it is for the Ruler's niece to oppose The Way Things Are."

"Oh, it's your aunt who's Ruler now," Beth said as the connection clicked into place. "That's why I thought she looked familiar."

"Yes, the previous Ruler was killed just over three years ago. We still don't know what happened. Aunt Lillian was voted in, but not everyone wanted her as Ruler. There was public disagreement and fighting. It was all a bit messy." Delphine sighed. "You really do have a lot to catch up on, don't you."

Beth rolled her eyes. "Don't remind me. Here I am, sixteen years old, and I have to do control lessons like a five-year-old."

"Well, don't think about it now. Come, let's dance." Delphine grasped Beth's hand and tugged her toward the pool, where several women were twirling and giggling and splashing. Perhaps it was Delphine's willingness to include her that made Beth feel more confident than before. Whatever it was, she let Delphine lead her to the edge of the water.

But then the copper-haired beauty slowed. She looked over her shoulder at Beth, an odd expression growing on her face. She frowned and raised her free hand to her forehead.

"Delphine? What's wrong?"

"I don't know." Delphine stood still, breathing slowly and purposefully, as if each breath caused her great effort. "I feel so … faint."

Abruptly, something changed. Pure, raw power—delicious and head-rushing and addictive—shot through Beth's body. Delphine's breaths became gasps. Her hand slipped out of Beth's, she stumbled a few steps backward, and then, amidst a rising chorus of screams, her limp body collapsed into the water.

* * *

"How dare you?" her mother hissed. "How *dare* you? Using energy-drawing magic against another siren? It shouldn't even be *possible*."

"Is she okay?" Beth asked, her shaking fingers pressed against her mouth. "Please tell me she's okay."

"She'll live," Lillian stated, marching into Evaline's sitting room. "Explain yourself," she directed at Beth. "How did you do that?"

"I—I just touched her. I didn't plan it, it just happened."

"Lies," Evaline spat. "That isn't how our power works. Even you know that. You'd been taught the basic laws of our magic by the time you left here."

Beth did know that. She knew exactly how siren magic worked—which was why she'd wanted to point out to Zoe that *eating* men had nothing to do with the way sirens obtained their energy. But she thought back over the past day, remembering each person she'd encountered, and realized it wasn't a lie. When Evaline hugged her on the beach yesterday, she'd touched Beth's jacket, not her skin. *Jack's jacket*, a voice reminded her silently, but she pushed the thought away. Lillian had touched her hair last night, and this evening, Evaline's hand had rested against Beth's back where the soft blue fabric covered her skin. And finally, when Delphine had greeted her, she'd touched Beth's sleeve. It was only when Delphine took her hand and pulled her to the water that everything had gone wrong.

"I'm not lying." Beth wrapped her arms around herself as she began shivering, from cold or shock or both. "Delphine was the first person to touch my bare skin since I arrived here. That must be how it—"

"It doesn't work that way," Evaline snapped.

"It's easy enough to test," Lillian said. "Bring another girl in. And stop that ridiculous shivering." She grabbed a shawl from the chaise longue and threw it at Beth, who drew it quickly around her shoulders. Two of Lillian's guards must have been just outside the room, awaiting orders, because they appeared less than a minute later, leading a scared young girl between them. "Touch her," Lillian commanded.

"What?" Beth recoiled. "No, I don't want to hurt—" But Lillian grasped the girl's hand, raised it, and pressed it against Beth's cheek. For a moment, nothing happened, and Beth almost laughed out loud in relief. But then the girl's eyelids fluttered and her breathing became shallower. She staggered and fell to her knees. The guards came forward and dragged the terrified, gasping girl from the room.

"What is *wrong* with you, Beth?" Evaline demanded. "Turn it off!"

"I can't!"

"Of course you can turn it off. You're a siren. You choose

when to exert your influence or power over someone else."

"But … how?"

"By simply willing it! Goodness, Beth, it's not that hard. This is instinct, not something that requires training. You touch a man, and you either want his energy or you don't. It's as easy as that to switch it on and off."

"You're missing the point, Evaline," Lillian said quietly. "She should not—*should not*—be able to draw power from any female. That is of far greater concern than her inability to control her power."

"It hadn't exactly escaped my notice," Evaline muttered, pacing between Lillian and Beth.

Lillian clasped her hands together. "Let us not forget that she is a halfling. Their magic—if they have any—can often manifest in unusual ways."

"*Unpredictable*," Evaline growled. "That's the word everyone likes to use."

Lillian sighed. "I hate that word."

Evaline surveyed her daughter, then reached for her. "Take my hand. This time, tell yourself that you don't want to draw any energy. Remind yourself that you are satisfied, in this moment, with what you have. It's as easy as that."

Beth slowly shook her head. "I don't think that will help. I never wanted to take anyone's power, so how will telling myself not to want it make any difference?"

Evaline made an annoyed sound at the back of her throat. "Perhaps you *subconsciously* wanted their energy. You are half-siren, after all, and my daughter. The desire for power should be strong within you."

Lillian's stern gaze flicked toward Evaline, and her eyebrows pinched together slightly. Beth wondered briefly what subtext she was missing between the two women, but now was not the time to ponder the possible power struggles within the siren community. Beth focused on her mother and her outstretched hand. "I don't want to hurt you ... Mom." It was the first time she'd used the word in almost ten years, and she hoped it might have a softening effect upon Evaline. After all, the woman was offering to end up in a gasping heap just to help Beth get this horrible life-sucking ability under control. Surely that meant she cared, even if just a little bit.

Evaline's expression remained stony. "I told you to take my hand. It was an order, not a suggestion."

Pushing aside the hurt Evaline's words caused her, Beth focused on Jack instead.

I never wanted to hurt him.

I never wanted his energy.

I'm content with whatever power resides within my own body.

Then she took her mother's hand.

There was no delay this time. Life-giving energy flooded Beth's body. Evaline tore her hand from Beth's grasp. She stumbled backward and caught herself against the wall as she breathed slowly and heavily, one hand pressed to her chest. Her gaze, horrified and cold, slowly rose until it locked on Beth's. "I told you to turn it off."

"I can't!" Beth wailed. "I don't know what this is. I don't know how to stop it."

"So," Lillian said, her tone sounding final. "She can draw

energy from anyone, and she has no control over it. She's dangerous. Clearly she can't stay here."

"But ... I ..." Beth turned to Evaline but found her mother's expression as harsh as Lillian's. "You're saying I'll never be able to control this?"

"It should be easy, Beth," Evaline said. "If it isn't easy, then your magic isn't like ours and we can't help you. And obviously you can't stay here," she added. "You need to leave."

As pain swelled in her chest, Beth imagined the cracks spreading across her heart. Cracks formed by her father and now deepened by her mother. "But ... where will I go?"

"That isn't our concern. Return to your father. Go off on your own. It doesn't bother me as long as—"

Evaline's final words were lost as Beth turned and raced out of the house. Tears blinded her as she ran across the corridor and into the oval garden. She should never have come back here. Of course she wasn't welcome. Of course she didn't belong. And now, thanks to the sudden awakening of her deadly power, she didn't belong in the human realm either. She was—

A figure stepped out from behind a fountain, and Beth nearly smacked right into the girl she'd almost killed. "Delphine," she gasped, taking a few hurried steps backward. "I'm so glad you're okay. I—"

"What did you do?" Delphine asked.

"I don't know." Beth continued backing up as Delphine moved with feline-like grace toward her. She expected anger, outrage, but the girl seemed almost ... fascinated. A slow smile curled her lips upward, sending a chill slithering down Beth's spine. That smile was somehow more dangerous than anger. "I can't control it," Beth explained quickly. "It happens whenever I touch anyone, man or woman."

Delphine slowly advanced on her, like a cat preparing to pounce. Beth turned to run but found a bench behind her. She swung back around, clutching the ring on her left forefinger. The ring that had brought her here. If she turned it now, would it take her back to the human realm?

She twisted it.

One—Delphine raised her hands—two—and pushed a flash of blue light at her—three.

And in a glittering, spinning swirl of magic, Beth was sucked out of time and space and thrown into darkness.

CHAPTER FIVE

BETH LANDED HARD ON ICY, WHITE GROUND. BONE-CHILLING wind swept past her, lifting snow into the air and tossing it about in gusts of misty white. With shaking fingers, she tugged the shawl closer. She climbed carefully to her feet, which already ached from the cold. Turning slowly, she took in the harsh environment. Steep slopes, jagged mountain peaks, distant trees she could barely make out through the blizzard, and not a single living being in sight.

How had she ended up on this bleak and lonesome mountainside? Surely the ring hadn't brought her here. Evaline had told her years ago that it was enchanted to take her between the human realm and the sirens' beach. Shouldn't it have transported her home? With fingers stiff and sore from the cold, she reached for the ring—but the pearl atop the metal was a mottled ashy grey, and a narrow crack ran across it. She tried to twist it and found it wouldn't budge.

The reality of her situation settled over her with horrifying clarity. She was lost and alone with no way home, and the deadly power that had awoken within her could never be put to sleep. She could never touch anyone ever again. Never touch Jack. And the cold. The cold, cold, *cold* was everywhere. Her nose, her lips, her feet. She dropped onto the snow and crumpled in on herself. Tears burned hot against her frozen cheeks. She longed to feel Jack's arms around her, to hear his warm voice as he comforted her. *You mean everything to me, my beautiful scarlet lady.* "I'm sorry, I'm sorry, I'm sorry," she moaned repeatedly until her voice gave way and her lips continued moving in an endless, silent plea for forgiveness.

She was vaguely aware that her magic might have the ability to warm her, but if that was the case, she didn't know how to do it. Besides, she thought as her shivering ceased and the pain in her fingers and toes eased into numbness, it didn't feel that cold anymore. An enticing drowsiness tugged her toward sleep. She blinked slowly, trying to remember if there was a reason to stay awake.

Yes. There was a reason, and his name was Jack. Through the haze of falling snow, she saw him coming toward her. When he was close enough for her to see his smiling eyes, he bent down and offered her his hand. "My scarlet lady," he said. "I've come for you." She reached for him with her stiff, frozen hand—but the memory of her deadly touch surfaced at the last moment, shocking her to the core. She yanked her hand back. The movement sent her head reeling, and the blizzard spun around her in an endless spiral. She tucked both hands beneath her chin as darkness closed in on her, wrapping her in blissful numbness.

* * *

Light flickered across Beth's closed eyelids. A crackling sound met her ears, and a sharp smell—herbs?—stung her nostrils. She twisted her head, trying to get away from the over-whelming scent as she blinked past the blurriness of her sleepy eyes. She stilled as the herb smell lessened and her vision cleared enough to focus on shadows flickering across walls. Walls? Was she back with the sirens? No, that couldn't be right. There was none of the clean, white opulence of Evaline's home. The walls here were rough stone with tapestries and animal skins hanging from them. And she must be far from the warm climate of the sirens' home if a fireplace was necessary here.

"You're awake," a voice said.

Startled, Beth tried to sit up. It took her a few moments of struggling against her own weak body and the thick, hand-woven blanket wrapped around her, but eventually she managed it. A girl—a little older than herself, perhaps—moved to her side and sat on the edge of the couch Beth found herself on. Her mass of golden hair fell in waves over her shoulders, with thin braids peeking out here and there. "Who are you?" Beth asked. "And where am I?" Wisps of dark, snow-covered images tickled the edge of her memory. A figure she had thought was Jack but couldn't possibly have been him. "Are you the one who found me out on the mountainside?"

"That was my older sister, Malena," the girl said, her words accented. The corners of her ice-blue eyes crinkled as she smiled. "My name's Tilda. What's yours?"

Her name? Beth didn't know if it was tales from the human world that she was thinking of or a genuine lesson she'd been taught in her early years with the sirens, but she didn't think it wise to share her real name. She pulled the blanket tighter around her shoulders, concealing her necklace from view. "Scarlett," she said, telling herself to believe it so it would sound like truth and not a lie. "My name is Scarlett."

She heard voices then, women's voices speaking a foreign language, and she sat up straighter to look over the edge of the couch. She was in a kitchen, she realized. Battered pots and pans hung on the wall beside a large fireplace, and there was a table with vegetables piled on one end, and another table with a bench on either side. The couch and a few old chairs were gathered into a sitting area within reach of the fire's warmth. As she took in the scene, two women entered the kitchen. They were older than Tilda, but Beth could see the family resemblance. Similar facial structure and blonde hair. Their eyes, though …

"I'm so glad to see that you've woken," one of them said, coming toward her. The other woman hovered near the fire-place. "My name is Malena, and this is Sorena." She gestured over her shoulder to the second woman, who hovered near the fireplace. "How are you feeling?" Her accent was the same as the younger girl's, but there was something odd about her voice. Something like a deep, subtle reverberation beneath the feminine tones. As she moved closer, Beth realized what was different about her eyes: her irises were as black as her pupils, and only a little bit of white showed on either side.

Beth shrank away from the woman, stuttering, "I-I'm fine."

"You're afraid," Malena said. "I can see that. We'll leave you with Tilda for now. Would you like some food? You must be famished."

"F-food? What—what's in it?"

Malena laughed, revealing sharp, pointed teeth. *Pointed* teeth? Who were these people? "Never fear, dear girl," Malena said. "It is not poisoned. We don't wish to harm you." She patted Beth's leg through the blanket with hands that ended in nails as pointed as her teeth. "Eat up, stay warm, and we'll speak again in the morning."

She and Sorena left, and Tilda walked to the fireplace. "Who—what are they?" Beth asked.

"Witches," Tilda said simply. "My sisters and I are witches."

"Witches?" Beth struggled to remember what she'd heard of witches as a child. They existed and the sirens didn't like them—no one liked them, really—but that was about all she could come up with. "You're *all* witches?" she said tentatively. "But you …"

"I don't look like them?" Tilda said, looking over her shoulder with a small smile. "I haven't been through the Change yet. My time is still coming."

"So … you're not actually a witch?"

"I am born to be one. Witch magic runs through my veins." She waved at the pot hanging above the flames. It rose up and floated down onto the stones beside the fireplace. "But no, I am not truly a witch until I've been through the Change." She walked across the room and fetched a bowl from a cupboard.

"Where are we?" Beth asked.

"In the Dark North inside a volcano."

Beth wondered if she'd heard correctly. "A—a volcano?"

"Don't worry, we have magic keeping us safe. You should eat something," Tilda added, removing the lid from the pot. "You must be starving after being out in the cold for so long."

"I'm …" Beth had been about to say she wasn't hungry, but the smell that reached her as Tilda ladled stew into a bowl was mouthwatering. Something that smelled so good couldn't be poisonous, could it? Besides, if these witches wanted her dead, they could have left her out on the mountainside. She took the bowl from Tilda—being careful not to touch her—and ate the tiniest of mouthfuls. It was heavenly, filling her with delicious warmth.

"How did you end up out there in the cold?" Tilda asked, sitting on the edge of the couch and pulling her feet up.

"I don't actually know," Beth said between mouthfuls. "I don't know if it was the ring or someone else's magic." Before she knew it, she was spilling her entire story. Her date with Jack, her power awakening, returning to the sirens, accidentally hurting Delphine and realizing she could never turn this power off. When she realized how much she'd said, she looked down at her empty bowl in suspicion. She certainly hadn't planned to tell Tilda everything. Had there been some sort of truth potion in the stew? Some spell that loosened her tongue?

"I'm so sorry about all of that," Tilda said gently. "It must be so scary to have a power you can't control. I can help you if you want. I mean, if you're not in a rush to leave." She said it so simply, as if there were no question that she could help Beth. Rather the question was whether Beth *wanted* help.

"You—Did you say you can help me? With this ability I don't know how to turn off?"

"Yes."

If that were true, then of course Beth wanted help. She *needed* help. And considering that she had nowhere to go, she was certainly in no rush to leave. But she wasn't naive enough to think that Tilda would offer this help simply from the goodness of her heart. "What do you want in return?" she asked.

Tilda frowned. "You think I have a hidden motive?" Then she smiled and looked down at her hands. "Well, I suppose I do. I'm curious, you see. Your power sounds so interesting."

A warning sounded at the back of Beth's mind. "My power is dangerous."

"All power is dangerous, Scarlett," Tilda said, "if used with dangerous intent. But you shouldn't be afraid of it. It's part of who you are, and it's beautiful, just as you are. You should embrace it. Master it, instead of letting it master you."

Embrace it ... master it ... It was an enticing thought, especially since the one thing Beth wanted above all else was to return to her normal life. Not to Dad, of course. She'd happily say goodbye to him if she could find within herself the kind of self-assurance this girl Tilda seemed to possess. But she wanted desperately to return to Jack and Zoe. To live a normal life, never fearing that her magic might hurt either of them. "I do want to master this power," she said hesitantly. "I'm just not sure if ..." *Not sure if I can trust you,* is what she wanted to say, but it sounded rude and unfounded, especially when these women had rescued her from an icy death.

"The other thing," Tilda added, "is that it can be so boring here at times. My sisters are quite a bit older than I am, and it's just not the same as having a friend nearby." She smiled. "So you see. I am not entirely selfless."

Beth bit her lip, not wanting to be fooled by anyone but not ready to let go of the idea that a normal life could once again be hers. "Do you really think you can help me?"

"Of course. It will take a bit of time, but I have no doubt my sisters and I can help."

Beth nodded slowly. "Okay."

"So you'll stay?" Tilda clasped her hands together.

"I'll stay."

CHAPTER SIX

"COME ON," TILDA CALLED BACK TO BETH. "IF WE HURRY, we'll be able to see the sunrise."

Beth hastened after the fair-haired girl with the brightly lit glass ball in her hand as she led the way along twisting, rough-hewn tunnels. She had spent the night beside the kitchen fire, warm and comfortable until Tilda had woken her and told her to dress quickly. A pile of winter clothes waited for her on the kitchen table: thick pants, gloves, a jacket, and fur-lined boots. Beside the glowing embers of the fire, Beth had felt over-dressed, but now, in the stone tunnels, the thick clothing did little to hide the growing chill as she and Tilda headed for the frozen land outside.

They turned a corner in the tunnel, and the stone walls came abruptly to an end. Instead, they were surrounded now by pale blue ice. Tilda stopped, lifted the glass ball above her head, and allowed it to brighten further. They were no longer in a tunnel, but in a vast cave with a flat, gleaming floor of ice and a ceiling and walls that curved and bent as though water had been flowing overhead at the exact moment the cave had been frozen into being.

Awestruck, Beth found herself unable to speak. "It's pretty, isn't it?" Tilda said, moving forward once more. "During the day when the sun is up, light shines through the ice from outside. It's even more beautiful then." Beth took a tentative step forward onto the ice, and Tilda added, "Don't worry, you shouldn't slip. The soles of those boots are enchanted."

The soles may have been enchanted, but that didn't stop Beth from experiencing several wobbling, uncertain moments as she tried to keep up with Tilda. She passed pillars of ice and formations that looked like slides, as though streams had wound their way through the air before becoming solid ice. On the far side of the cave, by the opening they were aiming for, the light became more purple than blue. As they neared it, Tilda lowered her glass ball and squeezed it until it shrank to the size of a marble. She pushed it into one of her pockets as Beth stepped up to the opening and looked out.

A flat expanse of snow-dusted ice stretched before her, surrounded on all sides by snowy slopes rising into jagged mountain peaks. Streaks of purple and orange colored the sky, bathing the entire landscape in peachy pink light. "We're bordered completely by mountains, but there, through that gap—" Tilda pointed at the space between two mountain peaks "—you'll see the sun rising."

It was so beautiful, Beth barely noticed she was shivering. "Stunning," she whispered.

"Come on." Tilda reached for Beth's hand. "Let's run to the other side so you can look back and see the glaciers."

Beth paused, looking at Tilda's hand and remembering the last person she'd touched: her mother. She pictured Evaline's horrified face as energy had been forcibly sucked from her body, filling Beth with a rush, a high, an undeniable—

"It's frozen solid, I promise," Tilda said, misreading Beth's hesitation. "We can run and jump and dance and it won't break."

I'm wearing gloves, she reminded herself. *I won't hurt her.* She swallowed and took Tilda's hand—and nothing happened.

Tilda tugged Beth forward onto the ice. Beth stumbled a few steps before slipping onto her hands and knees, laughing at the same time. "Didn't you say these boots are enchanted?"

"Well, they do require at least a little bit of coordination on your part," Tilda said with a chuckle. "Shall we slide instead?" She pulled Beth to her feet, turned around to face the cave they'd just left, blew across her raised palm, and—

A gust of air whooshed away from them, pushing them toward the other side of the frozen lake. Beth squealed, throwing her free hand out to balance herself as she and Tilda slid backward. As they came to a slow halt, Beth lost her balance once more and landed on her backside. Her groan of pain was mixed with laughter. "You can definitely tell I'm only half siren," she said through her giggles. "I can't imagine my mother ever falling."

"I'm sure you'll become more graceful," Tilda said as she

helped Beth up again. "You're still growing into your new powers."

Beth dusted snow off her gloves and looked across to the other side of the lake where the cave entrance was. The small, dark opening was dwarfed by gargantuan pieces of ice above and around it, seemingly stuck together. "Are those glaciers?" she asked.

"Yes. We were inside a glacier cave just now."

"But isn't that dangerous? Glaciers move and break, don't they?"

"Not here. We enchanted them to stay this way."

Beth breathed out a sigh of wonder. "That must have taken a lot of magic."

"It did. Many powerful enchantments bound together over time. Malena did most of the hard work."

Beth looked around as she ran her hands up and down her arms in an attempt to stop shivering. "Do other witches live around here?"

"Not close enough that you'd run into any of them out here, but yes. The Dark North is full of witches. We aren't particularly welcome in the rest of the world." At Beth's questioning gaze she added, "Our magic is ... different. Other fae are afraid of it."

"Oh." Her words reminded Beth how much she had to learn of this world. "Do you see the other witches often?"

"Not that much," Tilda said with a shrug. "We aren't part of a coven, so we mainly stick to ourselves. It's just the three of us and my nephew, Thoren. Malena's son." She cast a glance at Beth's shivering form and shook her head in amusement. "Let's get back inside before you shake so much you fall over again. We can have breakfast and then start figuring out your magic."

Back inside the cozy kitchen, Malena's porridge warmed Beth all the way down to her toes. She sat quietly at one end of the bench, her gloves still on in case she accidentally touched someone. She listened to the easy chatter of the three women. They spoke mainly in English, probably for her benefit, but occasionally they'd slip into that foreign, lilting tongue full of rounded vowels and rolling R's.

Beth had almost finished her breakfast when heavy footfalls sounded in the stone tunnel just outside the kitchen door. She looked over her shoulder in alarm. Hadn't Tilda said it was just the three of them and—

"Oh, hey. You must be the girl I just moved out of my room for," said the tall guy who stepped into the kitchen. He met Beth's gaze through the long strands of blonde hair that fell across his eyes. A hint of a smile pulled at his lips.

"Um—sorry—what?"

Tilda jumped up and skipped to his side, saying, "Scarlett this is Thoren."

Beth repeated the name in her mind, wondering why she recognized it. "Oh. You're—the nephew?" For some reason, she'd been imagining a child, but Thoren looked as old as Tilda.

"Yes, this is my little nephew," Tilda said, reaching up to pat Thoren's broad shoulder.

Thoren chuckled. "And this is my old aunt." He looped an arm around Tilda's shoulders. "So old that she'd barely been in this world two years when I was born."

Beth tucked her hair behind her ears self-consciously. "Did you, um, say something about moving out of your room for me?"

"Yes. All done," Thoren said as he moved to the table and sat opposite Beth.

"Oh, no, you don't have to do that. I'm happy on the couch in here."

"It's no problem," he said. "There's a storeroom my mother's been trying to get me to clean out for ages. She thinks I'll finally get it done now that the room is to become my bedroom."

A *storeroom*? Mortified, Beth rushed on. "No, please, I feel terrible making you leave your own bedroom. And I probably won't be here for—"

"It's been decided, Scarlett," Malena said with a smile that revealed her pointed teeth. She clicked her nails across the wooden table, and the rest of Beth's words died on her tongue. It wasn't worth arguing with a woman who could rip her eyeballs out with one swipe of her hand.

Her eyes flicked back to Thoren's for a moment, and he gave her another hesitant smile. "Best not to disagree with my mother," he whispered. "She likes to get her way."

CHAPTER SEVEN

"HOLY HAT!" BETH EXCLAIMED WHEN SHE SAW THE RIVER of molten lava flowing down the wall. She stumbled backward, expecting the molten rock to spew forth at any second and burn her alive.

"Holy hat?" Tilda repeated with a laugh as Beth backed into her and the bundle of towels she carried. "I've never heard that one before."

"Are you insane?" Beth demanded. "That's—that's—"

"The inside of a volcano?" Tilda supplied.

"Yes! Like, right here!"

"The lava stream and most of its heat are contained by magic." Tilda stepped past Beth and walked into the steamy room. "It's perfectly safe."

Not convinced, Beth hovered in the doorway. "Is it still safe when a person with no control over her magic is in the room?"

"Yes. The spells are stronger than you can imagine. And even if you were somehow more powerful, the spells themselves don't reside in this room, so you have no way of accidentally affecting them."

"I see." Beth took a few hesitant steps into the room. Three pools of different sizes bubbled up from beneath the stone floor, sending wisps of steam curling into the air. She loosened her scarf. "At least it's warm in here."

"I thought you'd appreciate the warmth." Tilda walked to the stone bench, moved a basket of bottles and soaps onto the floor, and spread the towels out before sitting down. "That's why I brought you here. The kitchen and workshop are warm too, but Sorena's busy in the kitchen today, and Malena doesn't like to share her workshop." She patted the empty space beside her and said, "Tell me about your magic."

Beth sat. "I know nothing. Let's start with that."

"Nothing at all? I'm talking about regular magic, not the magic that sucks the life out of people."

"I know," Beth said. "So am I. This magic appeared only a few days ago, remember? And after almost killing my boyfriend, I haven't exactly been keen to experiment with anything else magical. When I first got to the sirens, I was radiating magic everywhere. Odd things kept happening around me. But by yesterday afternoon, before the party, that had stopped. I don't know how, though."

Tilda let out a slow breath. "I see. This could take some time then. You'll need to master the basics of control before we can go anywhere near your ... unique ability."

Beth hung her head. "I'm sorry. I know I'm wasting your time. You probably have far more important things to do."

"Not really. I've been preparing for the Change, but in between my training, I help Malena and Sorena with their products. It's really not the most exciting way to pass the time."

"Products?" Beth asked.

"They make potions and salves and herb mixes and that sort of thing. Thoren does the deliveries every week to the stores that stock our wares, and I'm the one who gets left with boring tasks like labeling jars and counting the number of unicorn hearts we have left."

Beth waited for Tilda to start laughing, to say that she was merely joking, but of course she wasn't. Unicorns were real, she had to remind herself, and as foreign as it sounded, there were probably plenty of potions that called for unicorn heart. "Uh, that sounds very interesting," she said, hurrying to fill the silence. "Does Thoren have to travel far?" Picturing the vast snow-covered landscape outside, she imagined that the nearest form of civilization must be hundreds of miles away.

"All over the world, I think."

"Oh. So ... I assume you have magical travel methods like the sirens then?"

"Yes, of course. We wouldn't live all the way out here if we didn't have easy access to the rest of the world. We use candles. I'll show you sometime."

"Candles? That sounds ..." 'Impossible' was the word she wanted to use. "Impressive," she said instead.

"It is quite fun," Tilda said with a grin. "Anyway, the point is that you're not wasting my time. I want to help you. I have to be honest, though. I don't know much about what sirens can and can't do. But we can try things out and see what works."

"Don't forget I'm only half siren," Beth said, "so we can add that complication to the mix."

"You should at least be able to influence the elements, I think." Tilda leaned forward and gestured to the nearest pool. "Another reason for bringing you here. Perhaps you could try manipulating the water. Make a whirlpool, or get a stream of it to shoot up and arc over—"

"Tilda?" The two girls looked up as Malena appeared in the doorway. "I can't find the pixie's breath. Is it finished? I know you checked last week and said there was plenty left, but I can't find it anywhere."

With a long-suffering sigh, Tilda got to her feet. "I'll come and look for it." As Beth made herself more comfortable among the towels, Tilda looked back at her. "Don't think you're getting off lightly. I'll send Thoren to help you get started."

"Oh, okay." As Tilda and Malena left, Beth tried not to feel awkward about the idea of being alone in a room with a guy who wasn't Jack. A guy who might be influenced by siren magic she didn't even know she was using. It would be fine, though. She wasn't actively trying to seduce him. It wasn't like he was going to throw himself at her feet against his own will.

Right?

Ugh, please, no, she thought to herself as the alarming image crossed her mind.

"Scarlett."

What if the power to seduce men was also something she couldn't turn off? What if she spent the rest of her life unintentionally drawing men to her like moths to—

"Scarlett?"

She raised her head and found Thoren standing beside the pool, a questioning look on his face. "Um, yes, sorry." She had to remember to respond to the name Scarlett now. She could be Beth again when she returned home.

"Tilda said you might need some help with basic magic."

"Yes, please. If you don't mind." Beth's hands tightened together in her lap. "Yesterday I was apparently radiating magic everywhere, but now that that's stopped, I have no idea how to access it and make it do … well, anything."

Thoren sat down, leaving a respectable amount of distance between the two of them. "That's a good thing," he said, "the fact that you're not 'radiating magic everywhere,' as you put it. It means your body is already learning to keep its magic contained."

"If only the dangerous part of my magic would learn to contain itself too," Beth grumbled.

"You'll get there, don't worry. For now, focus on feeling your magic, pulling it together, and then directing it outward."

"Okay." Beth swallowed and tightened her hands in her lap. "Um, how exactly do I do that?"

He chuckled and pushed his hair out of his eyes. "It's difficult to explain. It's something we learn so early on that it becomes instinct before we even realize what we're doing."

"Instinct. Right. That really doesn't help."

He leaned back. "Okay, when your magic first appeared, did you feel different?"

Beth looked up, looked past those eyes almost the exact same ice-blue as Tilda's, and thought back to the night at the edge of the lake. "Yes. It was ... sort of like a hum that wasn't there before. I haven't thought of it much since then—I suppose because I became used to its presence so quickly that I forgot it was even there—but when I think about it now, I can still sense that faint hum."

"That's it," Thoren said, shifting a little closer to her. "That's what you need to concentrate on." Beth nodded, her gaze locked on his. "Focus on that hum. Imagine it as threads running through every vein in your body. You need to pull all those threads together into a core in your center—" his head seemed to move closer toward hers "—and then direct all that power outward at something—" his eyes flicked down to her lips and back up "—willing it to do whatever you want it to do."

Unable to look away, Beth nodded once more. Then, abruptly, she pushed herself to the far end of the bench. "I'm sorry. This is weird. I know I'm supposed to be able to exert my siren influence over you and make you do anything I please, but I don't know how, which means I don't know if I'm doing it right now. I don't know if you're sitting next to me because you want to or because my magic is compelling you to, but—"

"Scarlett," he said. "Stop. I'm immune, okay?"

She hesitated. "Immune?"

"Yes, I put a charm on last night to prevent myself from

being influenced by you." He raised his hand to show her a thin leather band around his wrist. A small wooden shape hung from it. He lowered his hand and added with a half-smile, "My mother thought it would be a good idea."

"Oh. That's—that's good."

"So, yes. I am sitting next to you because I want to."

"Okay." Did that mean he'd also been inching closer to her because he'd wanted to? Or had she imagined that part? Her gaze fell on the small space between them as she struggled to think of what to say next. Slowly, her eyes moved back to the charm hanging from his wrist. "Do, um, do men become witches as well?"

"Yes, although it's less common. The covens are still mainly female."

"Do you want to be one?"

"No. I don't plan to go through the Change. I'm tired of living here. I want to travel. I come and go a lot already." With a wry smile he added, "Now I simply need to convince my mother that she no longer needs my help around here."

"Hopefully she'll come around to your way of seeing things."

"Hopefully. So … do you want to give that magic thing a try?"

"Right, yes. Tilda told me to create a whirlpool, so I guess I'll start with that." She leaned forward and focused on the nearest pool. She did as Thoren instructed, reaching for that hum inside her, pulling it together and trying to push it out toward the pool. But no matter how much she focused on stirring the water around and around into a whirlpool, nothing happened. She tucked her hands under her arms and shook her head. "Is it supposed to be this hard in the beginning?"

Instead of answering her, Thoren said, "Tell me about each time you've used magic. Any kind of magic, good or bad." She didn't know how that was supposed to help, but she told him anyway. When she was done, he nodded and said, "Take off your gloves."

She frowned. "Why?"

"I think you're afraid of what you can do, and that fear is holding you back. These gloves are keeping you from hurting anyone, but they're also acting as a mental block for the rest of your magic. Remove the gloves, and you'll remove that mental barrier."

Beth raised an eyebrow in doubt. "You're a psychology expert now?"

"I may have read a book or two." He laughed then and shook his head. "No, I'm not an expert. I could be completely wrong, but there's no harm in trying, is there?"

She chuckled but reached for the fingertips of her glove anyway. What did she have to lose? Perhaps these gloves did symbolize a mental block. She certainly felt far more attached to them than any other piece of clothing she'd ever worn. Once the gloves were off, she placed them on the blanket and returned her focus to the pool.

"Don't be afraid of what you can do, Scarlett," Thoren said. "You're not going to hurt anyone."

She stared at the water, concentrating fiercely on pulling the core of power from her center and using it like a giant wooden spoon to stir the water. *Spin around*, she commanded silently. *Spin around and around and around.*

"Perhaps don't focus quite so intently," Thoren said, a touch of amusement in his voice. "You don't want to cause some kind of explosion when you do eventually release some magic."

She breathed deeper and forced her frown into a neutral expression, but the pool remained as undisturbed as before. "I can't do it," she said, flopping back against the wall in defeat and releasing all her built up tension.

And right in front of her, the water rose up in waves that spun around one another before crashing back down. Beth sat forward in amazement, watching water slosh out of the pool and across the stone floor as the choppy surface slowly returned to normal. She turned her head and beamed at Thoren. "I did it."

He smiled back at her. "I had no doubt that you would."

CHAPTER EIGHT

DURING THE DAYS THAT FOLLOWED, UNDER TILDA AND Thoren's guidance, Beth continued to test her magic. She didn't see much of the older two sisters other than at meals, but Tilda and Thoren were easy to get along with. Their magic lessons took place anywhere and everywhere. Out on the snow, in the kitchen, in the lava room, even sometimes in Malena's workshop when Malena wasn't using it.

Beth was both intrigued and intimidated by the workshop. The numerous hanging plants made her feel at home, but the animal skulls, eyeballs, and other strange ingredients often sent a chill crawling up her spine. The walls were lined with timeworn wooden shelves, drawers, and cupboards, all packed with ingredients, apparatus and books. A large workbench with decades' worth of dirt pressed into the grooves took up the center of the room. A desk as weather-beaten as the rest of the furniture stood against one wall, and an old couch—for Malena's clients to sit on while meeting with her, Tilda said—was angled next to it. Beth could have spent hours wandering around the workshop, examining every fascinating inch, but she went only where Tilda told her to go, and did what Tilda told her to do. The workshop was clearly Malena's domain, and she didn't dare step a toe out of line when she was in there.

It was slowly becoming easier to manipulate the earth, air, fire and water around her, although the elements didn't always respond in quite the way she'd planned. A sweep of her hand might bring about a mini tornado instead of a gust of wind, and a snap of her fingers might produce a fireball instead of a single flame. But she was definitely getting better. Beyond the manipulation of the elements, Tilda wasn't sure what Beth should and shouldn't be able to do as a half-siren, so many of their lessons consisted of Tilda asking Beth to try various things. 'Can you cut a slice of bread by simply thinking about it?' or 'Can you shrink your gloves?' or 'Can you shoot a spark of magic from your fingers and transform it into a bird?'

Beth tried everything. Sometimes magic happened and sometimes it didn't, but she learned something new in every lesson, and every night she fell asleep looking forward to the next day. She felt herself coming alive as she uncovered, bit by bit and day by day, more of the person she was meant to be.

* * *

They were in the kitchen two weeks after her arrival, practicing blowing air across their palms and watching it turn into smoke. Beth soon realized she could produce smoke directly from her fingertips without having to blow any air. "I can't see how this would ever be useful," she said as she waved her arms in slow, random patterns above her head, "but it's certainly fun." She twisted in a circle on the spot as smoke drifted from her fingertips. It gathered around her legs in a swirling spiral, floating slowly down to her feet and building in layers up to her hands. "This would make such a pretty dress," she said, "if it were possible to make clothes from smoke."

Tilda stopped blowing rings of smoke across her palm and tapped her chin. "Perhaps it is possible. I think I shall try."

"What are you doing?" The two of them turned and found Sorena, usually the quietest sister, standing in the kitchen doorway looking horrified. She placed her hands on her hips before demanding, "Where is your brain, Tilda? Smoke spells inside? I thought the kitchen was on fire."

"Relax, Sorena. It's dispersing already."

"Yes, into the rest of the tunnels. Our entire home is going to smell of smoke."

"Well, it sort of smells like smoke already," Tilda muttered. "We have fires going all the time." Sorena's lips pressed firmly together. Tilda groaned. "Fine. I'll do that expunging spell."

Sorena's shoulders relaxed a little. "Thank you. Please get it done before lunch." She strode away from the kitchen.

Beth raised an eyebrow and said, "I thought Malena was the bossy one."

"Sorena has her moments," Tilda said as she rolled her eyes.

"Thankfully they're few and far between." She looked around the kitchen. "Okay, I'll start gathering the things we need from here. Can you go to Malena's workshop and ask her for a small wooden block?"

"Uh, okay." As she left the kitchen and headed for Malena's workshop, she felt a twinge of anxiety. She'd never been alone in a room with Malena or Sorena, and she had hoped to keep it that way. They'd been friendly enough toward her, and while she was now accustomed to the subtle reverberation of their voices, their black eyes still freaked her out and their pointed teeth were more than a little threatening.

She knocked on the workshop door and waited until Malena shouted for her to enter. She pushed the door open and walked in. Malena was standing at her workbench's stovetop tending to a boiling pot—but she wasn't alone. Sitting on the couch near the desk was a stern woman with hair that was, interestingly enough, both blonde and green. A young boy nestled against her side. "Oh, I'm so sorry," Beth said. "I didn't realize you—"

"It's not a problem at all," Malena said with a wide smile that showed off her magnificently sharpened teeth. "Please come in. I was about to call for you anyway."

"Oh." Confused, Beth paused for a moment before closing the door behind her.

"Madame Lucia," Malena said to the woman, "this is Scarlett, my newest apprentice. I would like her to observe the watcher spell on your son. With your permission, of course."

Apprentice? Beth thought. Both she and Malena knew she was nothing of the sort, but she didn't dare contradict the witch.

Madame Lucia pursed her lips, then said, "I suppose it doesn't matter."

"Wonderful." Malena motioned for Beth to join her at the workbench. "You can add the magnolia bark to this pot, Scarlett. Stir for a minute, then strain the liquid into a cup."

Terrified of doing something wrong, but excited at the prospect of observing a real spell in action, Beth forced herself to approach the bench. On one side, atop the stove, grayish liquid bubbled within a small pot. Spread out across the bench were numerous bottles, vials, cloths and scattered herbs, but Malena had pointed to the bowl containing bits of a rough, dark substance. Beth assumed it must be grated magnolia bark. She picked up the bowl and whispered to Malena, "All of it?" Malena nodded, and Beth tipped the grated bark into the pot. She picked up the wooden spoon balancing across the handle and stirred the liquid. Should she count to one minute now? Had Malena meant exactly one minute, or was that simply an estimation? She was about to ask when Madame Lucia loudly instructed her son to stop kicking his feet against the furniture.

"Also add a drop of midnight spider venom," Malena added in a low voice, nodding to a vial containing a dark blue liquid. Beth's eyes flicked toward Madame Lucia, but the woman hadn't noticed Malena's instruction. Beth opened the vial and allowed a single drop to fall into the pot. It sizzled as it hit the potion's boiling surface. She stirred the concoction once more, and Malena, who was busy swirling a flask of liquid as black as soot, said, "You can strain it now."

Beth's eyes darted across the workbench surface and found a sieve. And there was the cup Malena had mentioned. Wrapping a cloth around the handle to keep from burning her hand—her glove surely wouldn't be thick enough to protect her—Beth lifted the pot and poured the contents over the sieve and into the cup. Bark, herbs and leaves gathered in the wire mesh, leaving a smooth blue-grey potion in the cup.

"We're ready," Malena announced, and Madame Lucia turned her attention back to the witch. "Bring the potion," Malena said to Beth as she carried her flask and a quill across the room. She sat on a low table across from the boy while Beth stood awkwardly beside her.

The boy took in the sharp tip of the quill with wide eyes and asked, "Will it hurt?"

"Not at all," Malena said. She nodded for Beth to hand him the cup and added, "Drink this."

With shaking fingers, the boy took the cup and sipped the contents. His face twisted as he swallowed, but he finished the remaining liquid and returned the cup to Beth's hand. Barely a second passed before he slumped back against the cushions, his eyes sliding shut and his head drooping to the side. Madame Lucia turned her accusing gaze on Malena. "What is the meaning of—"

"I lied, I'm afraid," Malena said. "The mark will hurt a great deal, which is why I put him to sleep. He won't feel a thing, and the pain will be gone by the time he wakes."

Madame Lucia hesitated, but her eyes remained narrowed as they looked Malena up and down. "You could have warned me."

"My apologies," Malena said, but as she caught Beth's eye she smiled discreetly, and Beth knew she didn't feel sorry at all for startling the woman. "Where would you like the mark to be placed?"

"Does it make any difference to the effectiveness of the spell?"

"No."

"Then … on the side of his torso, beneath his arm. I obviously don't want anyone to know it's there."

"Of course. Please lift his clothing."

As Madame Lucia moved the boy onto his side and pulled his shirt out of the way, Malena dipped her sharpened quill into the flask. Then, with movements slow and precise, she drew an eye onto the boy's side. As her quill pressed into his skin, black ink tinged with red dripped down his side, looking eerily as though the eye were crying.

"A cloth, Scarlett," Malena instructed as she finished the eye and sat back. Beth hurried to the bench and returned with the same cloth she'd used to pick up the pot. Without sterilizing the cloth in any way, Malena wiped it across the boy's skin, cleaning away the excess ink and leaving the perfect dark outline of an eye. Germs and infection clearly weren't a concern when magic was involved.

Malena then pressed her hand flat against the tattooed shape, closed her eyes, and began reciting words Beth didn't understand. She assumed at first that it was the same language she'd heard the witches speak before, but it sounded different. Hard edges and guttural sounds. As she spoke the final word, her hand tensed, her nails dug into the boy's skin, and a flash of light blazed briefly from beneath her palm.

Then she stood, wiped her hand with the cloth, and said, "That's it. Leave the shirt up for a few minutes to let the wound heal." She walked to her desk and sat in the chair, crossing one leg neatly over the other. "The other half of the spell has already been performed inside this book, as you previously requested." She moved a tattered old journal to the edge of her desk and patted it. "You'll be able to see and hear everything he sees and hears. Now, let's settle the payment while the sleeping potion wears off. Scarlett, please watch the boy until he wakes."

Beth kept her eyes on the boy as Malena and her client spoke in low tones behind her. She peeked over her shoulder at one point, expecting to see an exchange of coins or Madame Lucia writing a check—did checks even exist in this world?—but instead she saw the woman holding a vial against her temple where a faint wispy whiteness flowed straight out of her skull.

Beth turned her head back quickly, hoping neither of the women had seen her looking. The boy began to stir, and Beth, noticing that the eye-shaped wound had now healed, leaned forward and pulled his shirt down so the poor child could at least wake up fully clothed. "Mama?" he said as he sat up, blinking slowly and frowning.

"All done, dear," Madame Lucia said. She crossed the room and took her son's hand. "Is there anything else I need to know?" she asked Malena.

"No, but if you have any problems with the spell, don't hesitate to let me know."

Madame Lucia nodded as she removed what looked like an emerald encrusted pen from her coat pocket. She walked to the door, but instead of opening it, she lifted the pen and wrote on the wood surface. Beth couldn't make out the words, but they seemed to glow faintly before disappearing. And then, right before her eyes, a dark void of space began to form at the center of the door. It spread outward like ink bleeding into paper until there was almost no door left. Without another word, Madame Lucia and her son walked into the darkness, which swallowed them up within seconds before quickly pulling back together and vanishing as if it had never been there.

Beth, her mouth hanging open in shock, looked back at Malena for an explanation. "Faerie paths," Malena said as she stood and returned to her workbench. "We can't use them."

"Oh, is that what that was? I've never seen one before."

"Candles are better," Malena said as she began to wipe the workbench clean.

Beth stood there awkwardly, unsure if she was supposed to leave or stay now. She wouldn't relax until she was out of Malena's presence, but she was curious …

Malena looked up with a hint of a smile on her lips. "Do you have a question, Scarlett?"

She did, and Malena knew it. Malena always seemed to know these things. "Why did you tell the woman I was your apprentice?"

"I doubt she would have been happy for you to stay if she'd known you'd never performed a spell with me before."

"But … why did you want me to stay?"

As though it should be obvious, she said, "I thought it would be good for your education to observe one of our spells."

Beth nodded slowly. She supposed that made sense. Her

eyes fell on an open book beside the stovetop. Malena's spell book, no doubt. Curiosity getting the better of her, she moved to take a closer look at it. The words were in another language, but Beth could tell from the pictures that the page detailed the spell Malena had just performed. She looked up, a question in her gaze, and Malena said, "Go ahead."

She paged through the book, moving quickly past any pictures that seemed particularly gruesome. She felt un-comfortable looking at them, but it was probably just that she didn't understand all this magic yet. Whenever she saw a page with English notes written beside the foreign text, she stopped to take a closer look. "Sprite wings?" she murmured. "Is that a real ingredient?"

"Yes," Malena said, waving a whole lot of used apparatus into the air and across the room to the sink.

"Isn't that sort of ... wrong?"

"Have you met a sprite, Scarlett?"

"No."

"Nasty little things. Worse than rats. They're of far more use to the world as a collection of ingredients than they are alive."

"Oh." Beth added that to the long list of things she'd learned since arriving here. "Will I be able to do spells like this once I've learned to properly manipulate my magic?"

Malena gathered her scattered herbs and tied them together. "Not all of them—not the spells that specifically require witch magic—but some, yes."

Flipping back to the watcher spell and hoping it wasn't too out of line to ask, Beth said, "Why did Madame Lucia want this spell done on her son?"

Malena groaned. "She's a paranoid, overprotective mother. She's purchased numerous protective charms from me before, but now she believes that someone wants to kidnap her son. We put a tracking tag on him yesterday, and today's spell will allow the mother to see and hear what her son sees and hears whenever she looks inside that book. Poor child will have absolutely no privacy." She shook her head, then added, "But that isn't my problem. She is my client, and I must keep my clients happy."

Beth nodded, though she wasn't entirely sure she agreed with that. "Can I ask what the payment was for this spell, or is it confidential?"

Malena smiled knowingly, almost as if she'd been waiting for Beth to ask that question. "It wasn't too expensive a spell. A single memory was all I required from her." *A memory?* Beth opened her mouth to ask if that really meant what she thought it meant, but Malena said, "Time for lunch now."

It was then that Beth remembered why she'd come to the workshop in the first place. "Oh, Tilda sent me to ask you for a small wooden block. For an ... expunging spell?" she added hesitantly, hoping she'd got the name right.

Malena sighed. "Very well." She headed to the back of the workshop and bent down to open one of the cupboards. As Beth watched her, something in the far corner caught her eye. She hadn't noticed it before, perhaps because of the plants that had been hanging in the way, but something had since moved and she could now see a pedestal standing in the corner. A large glass case with a closed window sat upon the pedestal, and within it was a glass bell jar balanced on a cushion. Something

69

floated inside the bell jar. A flower? Beth walked slowly around the workbench, wanting to get a better look. It was a flower. A water lily, perhaps. Its petals were white with a pale blue tinge at their base, and it remained frozen in place in the air. "What is—"

"Come, Scarlett, it's lunchtime." Malena strode past Beth with a small block of wood in her hands. She opened the door and looked back, her nails tapping impatiently on the doorknob. "We don't want to keep the others waiting."

CHAPTER NINE

"SCARLETT, LOOK! I DID IT!" TILDA WALTZED INTO BETH'S room the next morning and spun around, her long skirt billowing around her. A skirt made of—

"Smoke!" Beth exclaimed. "It worked. That's amazing."

Tilda, almost glowing with pride, placed her hand on her hip. "I may not be a qualified clothes caster, but I can whip up a good enough dress when I'm feeling inspired."

"This is more than just good enough." Beth bent to take a closer look at the way the smoke of the skirt blended into the fabric. "Seamless. But won't you get cold with nothing to keep your legs warm?"

"I'm wearing stockings and boots under here. Besides, the smoke provides more insulation than you'd think. And even if I do end up cold, who cares? Not me when I'm dressed in something this amazing."

"Hopefully that thought will keep you warm then," Beth said with a laugh.

"And guess what else," Tilda added. "I made you one too." She turned and swept from the room before Beth could say another word.

Beth returned to the bed and finished pulling the blankets straight. Her elbow knocked Thoren's hourglass off the little stool that stood beside the bed, but her magic managed to freeze it in the air before it struck the ground. Pleased with herself for successfully employing useful magic, she replaced the hourglass on the stool. The hourglass was enchanted, of course, like many of the items in the witches' home. Not only did it give off a dim glow so she could read the time even in the dark, but after the sand had flowed past all twelve marks, the hourglass would automatically spin around and begin again to mark the passing of the next twelve hours.

"Here it is," Tilda announced, returning with a bundle of black smoke in her arms. "Try it on."

Beth didn't need to be told twice. She stood behind the wardrobe door and stripped her warm winter clothing off. After stepping into the dress and pulling it up, she looked into the mirror and—"Okay, why is mine so much more revealing than yours?" she demanded. "This neckline is far too low."

"Because, dear Scarlett, you are stunning and you should show off your magnificent beauty."

Beth snorted. "I'd hardly call it magnificent. And since when did 'beauty' become a synonym for 'cleavage?'"

"Scarlett," Tilda admonished. "I don't know what you see

when you look in the mirror, but I doubt you see yourself the way the rest of us do."

Beth huffed out a sigh. "Well, we can blame siren magic for that."

"You say that as if it's a bad thing."

"Isn't it?"

"Of course not. Do you need help with the laces?"

"Laces?" Beth felt the back of the dress with one gloved hand. "Oh, terrific. There are laces. This is basically a corset."

"It's basically stunning, is what it is." Tilda stepped around the wardrobe door and reached for the laces. When she'd finished tugging them tight—tighter than Beth felt necessary—she stepped back and said, "What do you think?"

Beth surveyed herself in the mirror. The gloves looked silly; they ended at her wrists and were too puffy to be considered elegant. For a strapless dress like this, she needed slim gloves that reached above her elbows. Satin, or perhaps lace, if she could find lace thick enough to keep her skin from coming into contact with anyone else's. The dress itself, though … Well, Tilda was right. It was stunning. But it pulled in her waist and pushed up her chest in a way that reminded her of the red dress. The one she'd worn for Jack. In a quiet voice, she said, "I can't wear this."

"Why not?"

Because only Jack should see me like this. Jack, whom she thought of less and less as each day passed. The realization filled her with immense guilt, and this dress only magnified that distressing emotion. "It just … isn't me."

Tilda raised an eyebrow. "You're a siren. You were born for

a dress like this." When Beth didn't reply, she said, "Don't you feel beautiful? Don't you feel like you could conquer the world in this dress?"

Slowly, Beth placed one hand on her hip and tilted her head. She swayed her hips so that the smokey skirt swished around her legs. She turned a little to the side and looked across her shoulder at herself. The thing was … she almost did feel like she could conquer the world in this dress—and she wasn't sure that was a good thing.

"That's right, Scar," Tilda said. "It's all about confidence. Find it and hold onto it and never let it go."

"How?" Beth murmured. She'd been searching for confidence her whole life, and it finally felt as though it might be within her grasp.

Tilda's reflection looked back at her. "I am independent. I am strong. I am *powerful*. Tell yourself that enough times, and you won't ever believe anything else."

"Is that how you were brought up? Being told to believe that about yourself?"

"It's how all witches are brought up."

Beth met her own gaze in the mirror as Tilda sashayed around the room. "I am independent," she whispered to herself. "I am strong. I am powerful."

"Scarlett?"

Beth looked up and found Thoren peering around her bedroom door. Well, it was technically his bedroom door. She still felt bad about forcing him into a storeroom. "Hi," she said, suddenly wishing she had a shawl to wrap around her shoulders. *No*, she reminded herself. Strong, independent, powerful. She didn't need to cover herself up.

"Uh …" Thoren stared, apparently having lost his voice or his train of thought—or perhaps both. Beth stared back with as much poise and self-assurance as she could manage.

Across the room, Tilda started giggling. "What happened to your protective charm, little nephew? I thought you were supposed to be immune to Scarlett's siren ways."

Clearing his throat, Thoren lifted his arm to show that the charm was still there. "I may be immune to the siren part, but I'm not immune to a lady's natural beauty." Tilda laughed even harder at that, doubling over while Scarlett felt her cheeks flush. She couldn't keep her own grin from pulling at her lips, though.

"I'm, uh, doing deliveries today," Thoren said, "and I wanted to ask if you'd like to join me, but, uh, I'll wait outside while you change." He ducked out and pulled the door shut.

"Oh, yes please!" Beth called after him.

"Who said she's changing?" Tilda shouted.

"I'm definitely changing," Beth said, reaching for the laces with her magic and coaxing them undone. "No way am I leaving the mountain in this dress."

"But it's a waste of a good dress if no one else ever sees it." Tilda dropped onto Beth's bed with a morose expression.

"We can think about letting the dress out of the mountain another time, okay?"

"Mm hmm."

"Hey, aren't you supposed to be at your assessment now?" Beth asked as she stepped out of the dress and picked up her warmer clothes.

"Soon."

"Will you be gone long?"

"Only a few hours. There isn't much left for me to be tested on. I should be ready for the next Change Ceremony."

"Oh, should I rather stay here and wait for you if you won't be gone long?"

"No, go with Thoren. It'll be fun for you to see some other parts of this world. Besides, Malena and Sorena are cooking up something super smelly in the workshop, so you probably don't want to be anywhere around here for the next few hours."

"I thought I smelled something unpleasant after breakfast." Beth pulled on her boots, wrapped a scarf around her neck, and closed the wardrobe door. "Okay, I'm ready to go."

She opened the bedroom door and found Malena storming toward her. No, storming toward Tilda, she realized in relief. "The High Tester just contacted me," Malena said to Tilda. "You're late."

"But I'm only supposed to be there in ten minutes."

"No, Tilda," Malena exclaimed, before launching into a string of words Beth couldn't understand.

Thoren stepped closer to her and said, "Ready to go?"

"Definitely." Malena was intimidating enough on a normal day. With fury rippling through her, she was positively terrifying.

The words echoed along the tunnels as Thoren headed for Malena's workshop. "Your language is so beautiful," Beth said, "even when spoken in anger. I wish I could speak it."

"I may not be able to grant you that wish," he said as they entered the workshop, "but I can help you understand the language."

"Really?"

"Yeah. There's a charm spell for that."

"Of course there is. There's a spell for pretty much everything, isn't there?"

Thoren shrugged and smiled. "Almost. I'll show you." He walked to the shelves above Malena's desk and pulled a box down. He reached inside, then held up a simple leather bracelet almost exactly like the one he wore to protect himself from her influence. Instead of a piece of wood, an off-white shape was attached to the leather. Bone or ivory, perhaps.

"Is this the way all your spells work?"

"All the charm spells, yes." He frowned. "Didn't Tilda tell you about them?"

"No."

"It needs to be something that can hold onto magical energy. Wood, ivory, a stone, a tooth. Something like that. This is a piece of pixie bone. The charm needs to be dipped into a specific potion—my mother has a whole box of pre-dipped items so she doesn't have to make a new one every time—and then you simply transfer energy into the item while saying the words of whatever spell you want to use." He wrapped his hand around the bone and spoke three words. The air seemed to ripple around his closed fist for a moment, and Beth assumed that was to do with the release of energy. "Here," he said, handing it to her.

"Thanks." The words to the spell had sounded simple

enough, so she repeated them as she pushed the leather bracelet onto her wrist.

Thoren, who had just returned the box to the shelf, looked back at her in surprise. "That sounded correct, actually."

"Would I be able to do this spell? Is it as simple as you made it seem?"

"Yes. You've got to make sure you have an excess of energy, though. Wouldn't want to run out of your own while doing spells."

"Oh, right." As he examined the dozens of vials and bottles lined up in rows on Malena's desk, she added, "So where do I get extra energy from?"

"Uh, other magical beings." He began packing the bottles into a wooden box so small she doubted it would hold even ten bottles. "I don't know the rituals because I'm not a witch. You'd have to ask my mother about that. Anyway, can you understand me?" he asked.

"Yes, because you're—Oh." Abruptly, she realized he'd been speaking a different language, and yet somehow, as impossible as it seemed, she could understand it. "Yes," she said with a laugh as she moved to stand beside him. "That's amazing. Why didn't Tilda give me a charm like this? It would be so much easier than all of you having to speak English around me."

"We don't mind speaking English. We use it for most business dealings."

"Wait, are you putting *all* these bottles inside that box? How are they ... Of course," she said, knowing the answer before she'd even finished her question. "Magic. It somehow makes extra space inside the box."

"Something like that."

"So where are we going for these deliveries?"

"Uh, let's see." He closed the lid and wiped his hand across the top. Silvery words rose from the depths of the woods and glowed upon the surface. Places, potion names, numbers. "We're stopping at two stores near the Pearl Strait, then we have a large delivery for the head healer at the Unseelie Court, then we'll stop at a store operating in the non-magic realm in Grimstad, Norway, and last on the list is Creepy Hollow, where we have one personal delivery and one store delivery."

"Ooh, the Unseelie Court? How exciting. Creepy Hollow sounds ominous, though."

"It can be." Thoren placed the box into a leather satchel, then opened one of the desk drawers and removed a black candle. "You might wind up with your heart ripped out by some terrifying magical beast." Beth blinked, unsure whether to believe Thoren. He lit the candle with a snap of his fingers. The resulting flame was a brilliant white. He looked at her over the top of the flame. "Just kidding. I'll be there to rescue you if something like that happens."

"How comforting," Beth said, wondering if she ought to stay at the mountain after all. She didn't get the chance to change her mind, though, because Thoren took her hand, held the candle up between the two of them, and with a blinding white flash, everything vanished.

CHAPTER TEN

Traveling by candle was a stranger feeling than traveling with the enchanted ring Beth's mother had given her. Her skin burned as she fell through bright white nothingness, as if the flame itself wrapped around her. The moment she felt ground beneath her feet once more, the discomfort vanished. The periphery of her vision filled with orange-pink sunset skies on her right and a rock face rising steeply on her left. She blinked at the black candle Thoren still held up between them, now an inch or so shorter than it had been. "Wow. That was … different."

Thoren let go of her hand and put the candle away. "Sorry, it's difficult to be exact when traveling long distances. We'll need to walk a half mile or so to get to our first stop."

Beth stared up at the pearlescent rocks shimmering in the

afternoon light, then out to the narrow stretch of sea on her right and the cliffs on the other side of the water. "That's okay," she murmured. "I don't mind walking past this."

They ended up on a pier beside a bay where a large community of fae lived on boats. The first delivery went to one of the makeshift stalls set up on the pier itself, and the second to an unfriendly old woman on a dilapidated boat who seemed eager to conduct business as quickly as possible before disappearing below deck.

Beth was excited for the third delivery, hoping she'd get to catch a glimpse of the Unseelie Court. She remembered her mother's tales of the court's lavish beauty and the vibrant color of the faeries that filled its halls. How thrilling it would be if she could see it all for herself. Sadly, she and Thoren ended up meeting the head healer at a dingy tavern somewhere, which wasn't nearly as interesting.

The hour or so they spent in Grimstad was odd. Beth felt the difference in the air around her, so dead, so still, so utterly lacking in magic. She thought of Jack and Zoe, and even of her father. She didn't care that she'd left the man who never loved her, but guilt gnawed at her insides whenever she pictured the two people she'd been closest to for years. The two people she'd simply abandoned. But she wasn't ready to see them again. She wouldn't be ready until she knew she'd never hurt them. So she put the thought of them from her mind as white heat blazed around her once more and she and Thoren arrived at their final destination: Creepy Hollow.

Gnarled trees and tangled branches surrounded them as they walked toward a clearing bustling with activity. After pushing their way past leaves that cycled through rainbow colors and climbing over giant mushrooms, they finally joined the crowd of faeries, elves, dwarves and other magical beings going about their daily business. There were open stalls, shop fronts built into trees, and archways that led inside the trees themselves. "I feel like I'm on the set of a movie," Beth said. "This is just unreal."

"This is your world now," Thoren said. "Time to get used to it."

"So where are these dangerous beasts you were referring to?" Beth asked. "Should I expect one to jump out at me at any minute?"

"They tend to stay away from the clearing. Wander off on your own, though," he added in a low voice, "and you're bound to come across something that thinks of you as a tasty treat."

She shook her head and laughed. There was probably some truth to his words, but she knew he was only trying to scare her. Thoren headed for one of the archways and walked beneath it into the tree. With no idea what to expect, Beth followed—and froze in the doorway with her mouth hanging open. There was a restaurant—an entire restaurant—contained within the circumference of this single tree. Did magic have no limits?

She hurried after Thoren, who ordered something from the bar before aiming for one of the booths in the back. "Who are we meeting here?" she asked as she sat next to him and removed her scarf. It was uncomfortably warm in here.

"Someone who calls himself Mr. A. He's never given us his full name."

Thoren removed the box from his satchel and placed it on his lap where it was hidden from view. He then pulled a book from the satchel. After removing several bottles from the never-ending depths of the box, he opened the book to reveal an interior empty of actual pages. He placed the vials inside and closed the book.

Just then, a man with a hood drawn over his head slipped into the seat across the table from them. "Ah, Mr. A," Thoren said, reaching across the table to shake the man's hand. "Punctual, as usual."

Beneath the shadow of the hood, Beth could see the man's gaze turn toward her. "Who's this?"

"Malena's newest apprentice."

Mr. A nodded slowly. He examined her for another few moments before turning back to Thoren. "You've got my normal order?"

"Yes." Thoren slid the book across the table. Mr. A took it and slipped it into an interior pocket of his coat, removing a flat silver shape the size of a credit card at the same time.

"You've ordered the drinks?" he asked as he slid the silver item across the table.

"Yes," Thoren answered. He pocketed the silver while turning to Beth and adding in a low voice, "Mr. A knows people in the community, so we have to make it look like a legitimate meeting."

Beth nodded, though she doubted any of Mr. A's acquaintances would recognize him with that hood drawn so far over his face. Thoren made polite conversation with him until their drinks arrived. Beth's tasted lemony sweet with a dash of something like licorice. She wanted to ask Thoren what was in it, but thought it better to wait until Mr. A wasn't around. He downed half his drink, then leaned a little closer. "I have a query about a different potion," he said. "Angel's Breath. Does Malena make it?"

Thoren lowered his glass. "She does, but we don't currently have any in stock. One of the ingredients—mermaid hair—has been hard to come by lately. We sold the last of our Angel's Breath this morning."

Mr. A steepled his hands and tapped his forefingers together. "So you don't know when you'll be able to produce more?"

"No. But you mentioned once that you have connections at the Unseelie Court. We've sold plenty of Angel's Breath to the head healer there in the past few months. You may be able to purchase some from her."

"I try to limit my contact with the Unseelie Court. Wouldn't want the Guild to find out."

"Of course." Thoren leaned back. "I'll ask Malena to let you know as soon as she's made more."

Mr. A nodded, then tipped the remainder of his drink down his throat. "Well, it's been good catching up," he said, placing the glass on the table, "but I must be on my way." He slid across the seat and stood up. "Until next month." And with that, he headed for the door and disappeared into the crowd outside.

"Right," Thoren said, leaving a few coins on the table and

standing up. "Only one more stop and then we're done for the day."

"Also in Creepy Hollow, right?"

"Yes, just a few trees up the road."

Beth smiled at how strange that sounded. Homes and stores and cafes all inside trees. This would take some getting used to. She placed her scarf loosely around her neck as they walked outside. "Does anyone else in your family ever do deliveries?"

"Tilda joins me occasionally, but not Sorena or my mother. Witches aren't welcome in ... well, pretty much anywhere outside of the Dark North."

"Oh." She stepped past two little girls—elves, she guessed—who were fighting over a doll. "I'm sorry."

"It isn't your fault," Thoren said with a shrug. "We do magic differently, and people are afraid of anything that's different."

She played with the tassels of her scarf, considering his words as they walked beneath an archway and into Phoenix Moon Supplies. The store was a brighter, tidier version of Malena's workshop, minus the workbench. Herbs, bottles, trinkets and charms lined the shelves. Several customers, including a familiar cloaked figure, were examining items and placing them in baskets. It was indeed Mr. A, Beth noticed as she passed him. He frowned at her and pulled his hood a little further over his face.

Thoren walked to the counter and rang the bell hanging from the beak of a brass phoenix. A woman shouted from the room behind the counter, telling him she'd be out in a minute. Beth joined Thoren and looked through the counter's glass surface at the knife display below. Beside the knives, in a bowl of water, floated a flower. With petals of white and palest blue, it looked almost exactly like the flower she'd seen in Malena's workshop. "Thoren," she said, "What kind of magic is that flower used for?"

"Hmm?" Thoren dragged his attention away from the knives. "Oh, the water lily. They're often used to house long-term spells. The kind of spells that need to last for months or years. People cast the spells and then transfer them into the flower. It's exhausting. Takes a lot of energy."

"So ... the one I saw beneath the bell jar in your mother's workshop ..."

"Ah, that one." He leaned his hip against the counter. "That flower holds all the spells that keep our home intact. Spells to keep the glaciers in place and to keep the ice cave frozen solid and to divert the lava flow away from our living quarters."

"So, not at all important then," she joked.

"Not at all," he repeated with a chuckle.

"Thoren!" A petite woman with spiked orange hair appeared in the doorway to the back room. "Sorry to keep you waiting. Come on back here."

The back room of Phoenix Moon Supplies was packed with boxes and shelves of goods. Extra stock, presumably. A ladder leaned against one wall near a small table, which Thoren walked over to. He placed his box on the table and began unpacking bottles and vials. The woman picked several of them up to check the labels and contents. She opened one, a vial with silvery sparkling contents that moved like liquid metal, and sniffed it. "Excellent," she said with a nod. "No one gets it quite right like Malena." She unlocked a wall safe with a wave of her hand and removed a drawstring bag. As she placed it on the table, Beth expected to hear coins clinking within it. Instead, the bag seemed almost to … move. As if something was alive inside it.

Just then, someone rang the bell on the counter. "I'll be back in a sec," the storekeeper said to Thoren. She left the room to assist her customer while Thoren finished unpacking the box. He returned it, along with the twitching drawstring bag, to his satchel.

Not entirely sure she wanted to know the answer, Beth asked, "What's in the—"

"Excuse me?" a loud voice enquired from the front room. "Where is the owner of this store? Miss Moonwood, is it?" Both Beth and Thoren looked around. A woman dressed in black from neck to boots with green in her blonde hair stood at the counter. In her hand she held a vial—a vial of silvery liquid that looked suspiciously like the vial the storekeeper had opened and sniffed.

"Damn," Thoren murmured, whipping his head back around and turning his back to the door. "She shouldn't have taken that out there."

"Why? What's wrong? Do you know that woman?"

"No, but I know she's a guardian."

"A guardian?"

"A law keeper. From the Guild."

"Are you sure?"

"Yes. I saw the markings on her wrists."

Beth peeked over her shoulder as the storekeeper nervously approached the guardian. "Is that a problem?" she asked Thoren.

"Potentially." He sighed, closed his eyes for a brief moment, and added, "The, uh, illicit goods are supposed to remain back here where regular customers—and guardians—can't see them."

"*Illicit?* You mean you're—"

"We need to go." Thoren reached into the satchel and drew out the witch candle.

Just outside the door, the storekeeper was feigning ignorance while the guardian said she needed to search the back room for other illegal potions. "Please don't make this difficult, Miss Moonwood. I don't want to have to force my way past you."

Thoren snapped his fingers and lit the candle.

"You're going to have to force your way through then because—"

"Hey!" the guardian yelled. "Stop right there!"

Thoren spun around with the candle in his hand just as glittering green sparks flew toward him. Beth shoved against his chest—and the sparks singed her gloves as they zoomed through the space Thoren had been standing in not a second before. He stumbled backward, the lit candle slipping from his hand and rolling across the floor. Miraculously—magically?— the flame didn't go out, but the guardian had already vaulted across the counter and was hurtling through the door. Beth and Thoren lunged for the candle, but a spray of water shot from the guardian's hand, dousing the flame as the three of them collided and fell to the floor.

"Run!" Thoren yelled as the guardian swung one leg expertly around his neck while twisting his arm back. But Beth was already yanking her glove off, already doing the only thing she could think of. She shoved her bare hand against the guardian's neck—just as a sparkling gold knife appeared in the guardian's hand and sunk into Thoren's side.

Thoren's cry and the guardian's gasp were simultaneous. The knife vanished and the guardian's grip on Thoren weakened. "What ... what are you doing?" she asked, fear flickering in her eyes as Thoren pushed her aside and jumped to his feet.

"Tora!" Another woman rushed through the doorway and ran to the fallen guardian.

"Stay ... back ... Raven," the guardian gasped.

"Run, Scarlett!" Thoren grabbed Beth's arm and tugged her to her feet. They ran from the back room and around the counter. Past the confused customers, through the door, around the tree, and into the forest. Leaves and twigs slapped at them, and the leather charm bracelet hooked on a low branch, yanking Beth's arm backward. She gave an angry tug, pulling her hand free of the bracelet, and continued running. When they'd put some distance between them and the clearing, they slowed to a halt. Thoren clutched his side with one arm while digging into his satchel.

"Illegal potions?" Beth demanded. "Are you serious? Tilda conveniently forgot to mention that part."

"They're not all illegal," Thoren panted, pulling an unused witch candle from his satchel.

"Oh, well that makes it all better then."

"Look, they're not bad potions. The Guild just has stupid, outdated rules about some of the ingredients." He snapped his bloodstained fingers, but nothing happened. He bent slightly, clutching his side once more, and held the candle out to Beth. "You do it."

Fear whispered at the edges of her mind. "Are—are you going to be okay?"

"Yeah, just light the candle. Think of flame and heat and releasing energy and—"

Beth snapped her fingers and a flame ignited. Brilliant white, instead of a normal flame, which must be due to the candle itself since she had no knowledge of how to produce different kinds of fire.

"Think of home," Thoren instructed. She wrapped her gloved hand around his wrist as she closed her eyes and did as he said. Bright light burned through her eyelids, and she knew it was working.

It was only as they made their way across the slick surface of the ice cave, her arm wrapped around Thoren as he struggled to keep moving, that she realized the word 'home' hadn't conjured up a single thought of her father's ramshackle house in Holtyn.

It had brought her here instead, to the place where—as much as she might wish to deny it—she felt more and more every day as though she belonged.

CHAPTER ELEVEN

"'SIRENS ARE ABLE TO TURN ON AND OFF AT WILL THEIR ability to persuade and influence men,'" Beth read out loud.

"Okay, so at least we know that for sure now," Tilda said as she lounged on Beth's bed, running her fingers through the smoke of her newest dress, a midnight blue one. She'd hunted through the shelves in Malena's workshop until she'd found a book—a children's one—that detailed the various magical beings of the fae world. The pages were yellowed with age and seemed to be gnawed at the edges, but Beth figured sirens must be the same today as they'd been when this book was written.

"But we don't know if *I* can do that," she said, "being halfling and unpredictable and all that."

"We need to find out. And if it's difficult, then you need to master control of it."

Beth, sitting cross-legged beside Tilda, shut the book with a groan. "Why? Can't we just move on to the one and only power that I absolutely *have* to gain control of? You know, the thing you said you could help me with when I woke up here two months ago?"

Tilda sat up and pushed her long golden hair over her shoulder. "I know you've been waiting a while. I'm sorry. But what's the point in mastering one thing if you can't master everything? And since sucking the life out of people will be the hardest part of your magic to control, we should leave it until the end, don't you think?"

"Yeah, I suppose so."

"Besides, what's the rush?" Tilda asked. Her grin turned sly. "I know you love it here."

Beth rolled her eyes and leaned back on her hands. Truth be told, she did love it here. It felt like home now, the ice cave and the warm fires and the cozy, fur-draped rooms. There were certain things she found disturbing about the witches' magic— the use of animal parts and the rituals for drawing energy that she still knew little about—but it was *magic* for goodness sake. She'd grown up in the human world, so of course she'd find this magic, and probably all other forms of magic, a little disturbing. And while some of the witches' ingredients might be illegal, those stuck-up guardians she'd heard more about from Tilda in the past few weeks really needed to get with the times and change their silly laws.

So she put any disconcerting thoughts from her mind and focused on what she enjoyed: learning spells; cooking food more delicious than anything she'd tasted in her world; playing in the snow with Tilda; curling up beneath thick blankets with the glow of embers warming her closed eyelids. "It is nice here," she murmured.

But Jack … He would always be her true home, wouldn't he?

"We should test out your persuasive siren ways," Tilda said, interrupting Beth's thoughts. "See if you can turn them on and off."

Beth straightened and looked around at Tilda. "On whom?"

Tilda raised an eyebrow. "Well, there is one male in the general vicinity."

Beth laughed. "Thoren, you mean?"

"Of course. See if you can *seduce* him," Tilda said with a giggle.

Guilt pricked at Beth's conscience as she thought once more of Jack. But this would be in the name of training, wouldn't it? It meant nothing to her. "You'll have to convince him to remove his charm."

Tilda climbed off the bed. "Something tells me that won't be difficult." As she headed for the door she added, "Put the smoke dress on. That'll work well. Not that you need the help. You could probably wear a sack and still win over any man you please."

"I'm only half a siren, remember?" Beth called after Tilda. She stood and crossed the room to the wardrobe. She pushed aside the normal dresses, coats and jackets Tilda had given her and found the smoky corset dress. She'd half expected the skirt part to disappear by now, but whatever enchantments Tilda had used kept the smoke drifting, swirling and curling without actually going anywhere.

She dressed quickly and used her magic to feel for the laces at the back of the dress. She closed her eyes and concentrated as she pulled them tight. She looked into the mirror and repeated the words she'd been saying daily to herself since the last time she wore this dress. "Independent, strong, powerful," she murmured. "That's what I am." She might be all those things, but she was also a little chilly with her shoulders exposed like this. She pulled a shawl from the wardrobe and placed it around her shoulders, tying it loosely below her neck.

At the sound of a tap on her door, she looked up. "Come in," she called. She twisted her hands together, feeling them grow sweaty inside her gloves.

"You owe me for this," Thoren said to Tilda as he walked in. He slipped the leather bracelet off his hand and gave it to Tilda. He turned to face Beth with an awkward half-smile on his face. "Uh, hi. So ... I'm the test subject for your Intro to Seduction class?"

A laugh escaped her lips before she could stop it. Thoren grinned, but his dear Aunt Tilda, leaning in the doorway, groaned and pushed him forward. "Take this seriously, both of you."

So Thoren pressed his lips together and waited while Beth tried to figure out how to be a seductress without giggling. "Well," he said after a few moments, "I'm not feeling the urge to fall at your feet and profess my undying love for you, so ... does that mean you need a little more practice?"

She wanted to groan and say that she would need a *lot* more practice to get this right, but Tilda had said to take it seriously and she was right. The only way Beth could ever return to her previous life was if she could master every part of her magic, and that included this part—no matter how silly it might feel.

She closed her eyes and breathed out slowly. *I am born to do this*, she told herself. *I am born to make men fall at my feet.* As her eyes slid open, she locked her gaze on Thoren's. With tendrils of smoke swishing around her legs, she moved slowly toward him. *I want you to want me*, she whispered within her mind. *I am the only thing you see, the only thing you want, the only thing that matters. You would do anything for me.*

"Thoren," she said quietly, tilting her head down before looking up at him between her lashes. "Would you walk naked into the snow if I asked you to?"

"I ..." He swallowed and nodded. "Yes."

"If I asked you to leave your family and follow me, would you do it?"

"I would."

"Would you throw yourself in front of an enemy to protect me?"

He nodded again. "I wouldn't hesitate."

It wasn't right, she told herself, this manipulation magic. And yet ... something about it was addictive. Something about knowing that he would do anything she asked filled her with giddying power. Never looking away from his eyes, she reached for the knot of the shawl and slowly untied it. She let the shawl slip off her shoulders and watched the way Thoren's eyes moved down her neck and across her chest. His gaze roved back up over her throat, her lips, and settled on her eyes. "I didn't see it before," he whispered, "but I do now. You are the most exquisite creature I have ever beheld."

He tilted his head closer to hers, his eyes on her mouth now, and she knew he wanted to kiss her. His pulse jumped at his neck, and her heart leaped to match its pace. Her eyes slid down to his lips, full and soft. She'd be lying if she said she hadn't thought of them before. Hadn't wondered, in the warmth of her bed late at night as she fell in slow motion toward sleep, what it might be like to kiss him. Fantasies that teased at the edges of her sleep-drugged mind.

Barely an inch separated them now as Thoren's magic-induced desire tugged him closer to her.

Time to turn it off, she told herself. *Turn it off before you hurt him.*

But she didn't want to turn it off. She wanted this, the kiss, *him.* This feeling—this heat that bloomed from her chest and radiated outward—had nothing to do with manipulation or magical influence.

It was real.

That awareness was enough to shock her to her senses. She stepped back, shutting down all feeling. Thoren blinked. He shook his head. He met Beth's gaze with uncertainty in his eyes. "You're … not doing it anymore, are you?"

"No." She folded her arms over her chest. "Why, do you still feel something?"

"No, no, just checking." He stumbled backward, almost knocking Tilda over in his haste to put some distance between himself and Beth. He took his leather bracelet from Tilda and pushed it back onto his wrist.

"That," Tilda said as Thoren hastened from the room, "was magnificent."

"Thanks." Beth turned away and bent to retrieve her shawl, hoping to hide her warm cheeks and the heaving of her chest as her heart took its time returning to a normal pace. She must have simply been caught up in the moment. She didn't truly feel that way about Thoren. She didn't. She *couldn't*. Not when she still had Jack.

Jack! Argh! The guilt chewed at her insides, making her feel nauseous.

"This is wonderful." Tilda clapped her hands. "You can easily turn this power on and off. I declare we should have a celebratory snowball fight out on the mountainside."

Tilda was right: it was wonderful. And the fluttering in her chest was almost completely gone, so it most likely meant nothing. Pushing thoughts of both Jack and Thoren from her mind, Beth turned back to face Tilda. "I second that idea." With a mischievous smile, she added, "I would very much like to throw a snowball at that perfect blonde head of yours."

CHAPTER TWELVE

THE ICY AIR HELPED TO CLEAR BETH'S HEAD. SHE AND TILDA skated across the frozen lake and raced each other up the snowy slope on the other side. They conjured snowballs and miniature blizzards and spinning tornadoes of snow dust. When they were well and truly exhausted, and the last rays of daylight were vanishing behind the tall peaks, they collapsed onto the snow. Beth removed her scarf and held it in her hands while stretching, pulling, and tugging at her magic, urging the scarf to grow bigger and bigger until it was as large as a blanket.

"Impressive," Tilda said. "You've come a long way."

"I don't think siren magic is supposed to be able to do this," Beth said, thinking of everything she'd read in the book Tilda had found, "but I'm not really a siren. I think I should embrace my halfling label and all the unpredictability it brings with it."

They sat on the edge of the blanket and pulled the rest of it around them, huddling together as the pinky purple of sunset shifted toward ink blue. "That's the first snowball fight I've had that was actually fun," Beth commented as they stared across the wintry landscape.

"But all snowball fights are supposed to be fun."

Beth chuckled. "Clearly you've never been to school."

"I went to school as a child. It wasn't so bad."

"Okay, clearly you've never been subjected to the bullying that takes place in schoolyards."

Tilda hesitated, then asked, "What happened?"

"Just … kids being mean. Throwing snow in my face and pushing me down. Those terrifying few moments where my face was pressed into the frozen ground and I couldn't breathe, and then forcing myself up, gasping for air, and finding everyone laughing at me because it was all a joke to them."

"Cowards," Tilda growled. "If only they could see you now. You'd whip that snow into a frenzy, into a blinding storm. They'd never know what hit them."

Beth nodded. "It's strange thinking of it now. Back then I felt so utterly powerless against children like them. I wanted to rage against them, to scream, to hit, to *hurt* them like they'd hurt me. But now I know that all it would take is a simple touch. One touch and they'd be on the ground, as powerless as I once was."

"Powerless is something you will never again be," Tilda murmured.

Quiet descended over them as they watched the night sky, a dark expanse scattered with more stars than Beth could ever have imagined existed. In the distance, above the mountain peaks, a faint green light, little more than a smudge, began to flicker. Beth leaned forward slightly, paying more attention as the light grew. Green tinged with pink and purple, climbing across the sky, bending and looping lazily as it continued to flicker.

"Amazing, isn't it?" Tilda said.

"Mesmerizing," Beth whispered. The celestial light show was more captivating and beautiful than any magic she'd seen since arriving in this world. "I sometimes feel," she murmured, "that I could happily live here for the rest of my days."

Tilda leaned her head on Beth's shoulder. "Perhaps you should. Nothing is stopping you from doing just that."

Beth sighed. "But I have to go back to Holtyn. I have to explain to Jack what happened. And Zoe. She was my best friend, and I vanished with no explanation." She looked down and found Tilda's eyes closed, a peaceful smile on her lips. "Don't you think I owe them that much?"

"Mmm," Tilda said sleepily. "Maybe. Maybe not. I don't think you owe anyone anything. You are the master of your own destiny, Scarlett." She raised her head, pointing her face to the sky as if to soak in the colorful night lights. "You can go anywhere you choose, or you can stay right here. You can wander the fae realm for the rest of your years, beguiling men with your siren powers, or you can live out your days in the human world as if magic had never touched you. Or you can stay right here in this frozen wonderland. You could even go through the Change like I'm about to do. Become a witch, fierce and powerful and perfectly in tune with the elements.

Your life is your own, Scarlett, and no one else will ever have the right to tell you what to do with it."

Beth touched the inside of the blanket, releasing a trickle of heat and urging it to travel through the woven fibers, warming the two of them as she considered Tilda's words. "Did you say I could go through the Change?" she asked quietly.

Tilda looked at her. "Yes."

"Is that allowed? Would it even work? I have no witch blood."

"Yes, it would work. Having witch blood simply means I am called to this life, just as having siren blood means you are called to the water. Our blood does not force us to walk a specific path, though. I could choose not to become a witch, and you could choose to stay away from the ocean."

"So ... you were being serious then?"

"Yes." Tilda peered more intently at her. "Are *you* being serious?"

"I ... I don't know. I want to be with Jack again, but I want my life to include magic. I want to have the kind of life you're going to have, but I want Jack to be in it. Is there a way I can have both?"

"Of course you can have both. You can have anything you want, Scarlett."

Scarlett. Why was it that she hadn't told Tilda her real name yet? She trusted Tilda now. The young almost-witch was her closest friend these days. She opened her mouth to say it—*My name is Beth*—but the words died on her tongue. Did it matter what her name used to be? Not really. Not when she had left behind that plain, shy girl who possessed no magic. Not when she had become so used to being Scarlett instead.

"So," she said, "if I had everything I wanted, how would that work? Where would I live?"

"You could live right here with us. You've seen how easy it is to travel. One flash of candlelight and you'll be with Jack. Or," she added as she saw Beth's frown, "you could do it the other way around. Live with Jack and work with us. The point is that you can come and go as you please."

"So this could really work?"

"Yes. Oh, this is wonderful." Tilda turned to face Beth fully, grasping her arms excitedly. "I don't know why I didn't think of it before. You're the perfect candidate. So many witch spells rely on the use of magical energy, and we have our own methods to draw that energy out of other beings, but you've got that ability built into you. You don't need a complicated ritual when you can take energy with your bare hands."

"True," Beth mused.

"So do you want to do this? Really and truly?"

Beth bit her lip, thinking of Jack and her magic and this exquisite frozen world she never wanted to say goodbye to. She didn't have to choose. She could have it all. "I do," she said. "I want to be a witch."

CHAPTER THIRTEEN

"WHAT EXCITING NEWS!" MALENA EXCLAIMED WHEN TILDA and Beth returned to the kitchen and Tilda shared the news of Beth's decision. Beth beamed as she hurried to the fireplace to warm her hands.

"I agree," said Sorena, her gentle smile hiding her pointed teeth. "It's perfect. We would so love to have you as one of us, Scarlett."

"I got dinner," Thoren announced as he walked into the kitchen. He met Beth's gaze for a moment, but she looked away quickly, annoyed at the sudden rush of her pulse. *Think of Jack*, she told herself. Jack, whose smile she *wasn't* forgetting. Whose eyes she could *definitely* remember the exact color of. She frowned at the flames, then startled when someone touched her arm.

"Can you help with dinner?" Malena asked. "It will be so much easier if you do it. I haven't wanted to ask you before because I thought it might make you uncomfortable."

"Uncomfortable?" Beth asked as she followed Malena to the table she always prepared food at. "Why is that?"

"Oh, just because I know that most humans don't kill their own food. It would be good for them if they did, of course. Everyone should know where their food comes from."

"I—uh—you're right. I've never had to kill my own food."

"No time like the present to get started then," Malena said. "What have we got tonight, Thoren?" she asked her son as he approached the table carrying a wriggling sack. Instead of answering, he dumped the sack on the table, and out jumped—

A hare. Spotless white, its tiny black nose twitching and its body shivering. Malena's hand came down upon it before it could move another inch.

"Why—um—why did you say it will be so much easier if I do it?" Beth asked.

"We have numerous ways of killing the animals we eat, both magical and non-magical, but some can be messy. You, however, need only touch it."

Of course. Finally, a use for her special power that didn't involve hurting other people. It would, unfortunately, hurt the poor hare, but it was necessary if she and her new witch family wanted to eat. She pushed down the urge to hug the creature to her chest and run her fingers through its soft white hair. *Food*, she told herself. *This is food, not a pet.*

"Well, come on," Malena said, "or it'll be midnight before we eat anything."

"I'll hold him down," Thoren said. "You can get started with the vegetables, Mom."

Malena moved to the mountain of vegetables at the other end of the table while Beth pulled one glove off. She hesitated for several moments, during which she reminded herself that she didn't want to appear weak or squeamish. She would be a witch soon, and there was no place for either of those things in her future.

Do it. Just do it.

As she steeled herself and moved in, Thoren's hand squeezed tighter around the hare. A muted flash of light pulsed from his hand, and the hare went limp. Thoren's eyes flicked toward Malena, but she was busy chopping carrots. "My mother can be a little pushy," Thoren said in a low voice. "She should have warned you earlier, given you a little more time to prepare yourself." His eyes rose and found hers, his cool blue gaze sending a pleasant tingle down her spine. "You can do it next time."

* * *

"We have much to do to prepare you for the Change," Malena said to Beth as the five of them sat around the table eating dinner. "You probably won't be ready when Tilda goes through the process in a few weeks, but certainly next time."

"Is it supposed to happen at a certain age?" Beth asked.

"Any time after the age of sixteen. Tilda could have done it four years ago—" Malena frowned at her younger sister "—but she enjoyed playing around too much to bother with the requirements for passing the preliminary assessments."

"What does it matter?" Tilda said with a wave of her hand. "I'm ready now, so let's not dwell on the past. Or," she added as she paused with her spoon between her bowl and her mouth "—I could wait until Scarlett is ready and do the Change with her."

"More delay tactics?" Sorena said.

"Of course not. I just thought it would be fun training with Scarlett." Tilda grinned at Beth over her bowl.

"We can talk about it more in the next few days," Malena said. "For now, Scarlett needs to start learning about the energy rituals. We can do one tomorrow night."

"She won't need to do those, Malena," Tilda said. "She can draw the energy herself. That's what will make her such an incredible witch, remember?"

Malena sighed through her nose. Foreign words rolled from her tongue at lightning speed.

Tilda dismissed her sister's annoyance with an eye-roll and faced Scarlett. "Malena says that *obviously* you need to witness the rituals so that you know how other witches draw energy. And, of course, you'll need to know how to release the energy from your body so it can be stored and used later on."

"Exactly," Malena said. "So we'll do one tomorrow night. What energy are we low on at the moment?"

"Human," Sorena said between mouthfuls.

Beth coughed as a piece of meat caught in her throat. She swallowed hard. "Did you, uh, say human?"

Sorena looked up. She finished chewing. "Yes. Mostly we use energy derived from magical beings, but there are a select few spells—important ones—that require human energy."

"Okay, we'll get hold of a human and perform the ritual tomorrow night," Malena said. "Scarlett, you can bring the human in. It will be good practice for you. For your siren influence. Actually, bring two men. You can use your own power to remove energy from one, and then observe the ritual to remove energy from the other."

Hoping she wasn't misunderstanding Malena, Beth said, "We won't draw *all* their energy from them, will we?"

"Of course we will," Malena answered. "We don't want to waste any."

"So you ... you want ..." Beth put her spoon down. "I'm sorry. We're going to be *killing* two men?"

"Yes."

"But ... that's wrong. We can't kill people."

"Why not?" Malena asked.

"Because ..." Beth fumbled for the right words. "It's ... just ... wrong!"

"According to whom?"

"I don't know. The guardians? Don't they have laws about killing people?"

Tilda chuckled. "I think we've already established the silliness of whatever laws guardians come up with."

"Scarlett, dear." Malena reached across the table and laid a hand on Beth's sleeve. "Did you have a problem killing the hare?"

Beth paused for a second before lying. "No."

"Why not?"

"Because we needed to eat it in order to survive."

"Exactly," Malena said with a nod. "Just as we need human energy to survive."

"We do?" Beth asked, wondering suddenly what fundamentally important spells she'd missed. She shook her head, refusing to be distracted. "But animals and humans are different."

"Not really," Sorena said. "They're both lesser beings."

Beth looked at Tilda to see if she agreed with this craziness. Tilda gave her an apologetic smile. "I'm sorry. It must be difficult for you to think this way when you've grown up among humans. But honestly … they're on a different level. A lower level. If they have something we need, then we have to take it. It's an adjustment in mindset, I know, but you'll soon see what we mean."

Beth highly doubted that. "What if we take less energy from more humans? That way we get the same amount of energy, but we don't have to kill anyone."

At this, Tilda looked upset. "But that would cause them unnecessary confusion and suffering. We don't want that."

"Is this going to be a problem, Scarlett?" Malena asked. As she waited for an answer—an answer Beth was too afraid to give—her expression turned kinder. "You need to accept that this is part of who you are, dear. You, more so than any of us, were born for this."

CHAPTER FOURTEEN

I WAS BORN FOR THIS, BETH WHISPERED SILENTLY TO HER-self. The thought did little to convince her, though. As far as Malena and her family knew, Beth had chosen the witch way. She had sat in silence at dinner last night until eventually agreeing out loud that humans might not, after all, be worth the same as magical beings. But her heart believed something entirely different. And now here she was, tasked with bringing in two men, and she still had no idea whether she would go through with it or not—or what her options would be if she chose to disobey Malena.

"Does it matter to you where these men come from?" she'd asked last night, planning to search for a prison full of crim-inals. Perhaps her guilt would be assuaged if she took the lives of men who didn't deserve to live in the first place.

"I'll find you a suitable gathering," Tilda had assured her, at which Beth had felt her heart sink even further.

The suitable gathering turned out to be a glamorous fund-raising event in some European city where no one spoke English. Not that the language difference mattered since Beth was supposed to be able to get men to fall at her feet without uttering a single word. As darkness fell and the tiniest of snow-flakes began to fall, she and Tilda snuck into the city hall with the aid of a back entrance and an unlocking spell. They waited in a side corridor, peering around a marble column at the guests entering the building.

"Why not something a little more discreet?" Beth whispered to Tilda. "I could find a pub down the road, slip in quietly, choose two men, and get them to leave with me. No one will notice."

"This isn't about being discreet. Quite the opposite, in fact." Tilda took Beth's gloved hand and gave it a reassuring squeeze. "You have no idea, Scar, the kind of power you could wield, and we want to show you that. We want you to fully embrace your siren side so that you can become the powerful woman you were always meant to be."

The powerful woman I was always meant to be.

The words had an intoxicating ring to them, and Beth couldn't help admitting to herself that she wished them to be true. If this was her path to becoming everything she was meant to be, then why not embrace it? Why not run headlong toward her destiny instead of shying away from it like a scared little girl? Her gaze fell on the nearest window, on the aged, rippling glass with snowflakes drifting through the air on the other side, and she remembered those children—those *humans*—pushing her down and pressing her face into the snow until her lungs screamed for breath.

Her decision was made.

"Okay," she said to Tilda. "I'm ready to do this."

"Wonderful." Tilda gave Beth's hand a quick squeeze. "I'll be waiting outside with Malena and Sorena. We'll be ready to begin the ritual as soon as you join us."

Beth stepped around the pillar and made her way toward the party. Through the wide doorway, she could see them all. The celebrities, the wealthy, the politicians, all chattering, laughing and sipping from their glasses of sparkling golden wine. She fit right in with her glamorous black dress. It was similar in style to the red dress, but longer and with a glittering shimmer running through the fabric. Black satin gloves that ended above her elbows completed the outfit. She'd looked in the mirror at home and seen someone else staring back at her. Someone older and confident and fully aware of her power.

Someone named Scarlett.

She wished she felt that assurance now as she stopped at the top of the stairs that led down into the crowded area. Instead, she felt suddenly ridiculous. She was a little girl playing dress-up in a room full of adults, and they would no doubt start laughing the moment they noticed her standing there. She considered turning and running. Running from this party, this life, this—

"No," she murmured before her feet could catch up with her panicked thoughts. *I am not scared and I will not run. I am independent. I am strong. I am powerful.* She pushed her shoulders back and breathed in slowly and deeply. She had nothing to be nervous about. She pictured herself the way she had always pictured her mother. She was breathtaking, she was captivating, and men would fall at her feet and worship her before they'd dare make fun of her.

She walked slowly down the stairs, gliding in a way she'd only ever imagined herself doing. She stared straight ahead, the smallest of smiles on her lips, aware of the heads turning her way but refusing to acknowledge them. Let them watch. Let them long for her gaze like dying men longing for water in a desert. She reached the bottom of the stairs and continued her slow prowl through the crowd. She was a predator stalking the herd, searching for exactly the right prey. She could feel their energy, their very essence, thrumming in the air. It called to her, and she *wanted it.*

I was born for this, her soul whispered to her.

She moved toward the edge of the crowd as people— women, most likely—restarted their conversations with murmurs and awkward laughter. She spotted two older men leaning against one of the many pillars that lined each side of the hall. They gaped at her, their lips parted as though they might have been about to say something before their words completely escaped them. She examined them—their silver hair and the lines that creased their faces—as she stalked slowly past.

You, she whispered in her mind to the two men who'd lived many years already. *You want to come with me. Nothing else in your world matters anymore.* She tilted her head to the side and gave them an alluring smile. Then she turned and headed for a side door she'd spotted, her hips swaying slightly as she continued her gliding motion. She glanced over her shoulder, and it filled her with exhilaration to see the two men following her, to know that whatever she willed, they would do.

She retrieved the fur-lined cloak and boots she had left beside the back entrance and pulled them on. She lifted the hood over her head, then led the men outside. They followed her through the snow to the outskirts of town where the witch sisters waited in the trees. By the time Beth reached the flickering green fire, the men were shivering and their hair and clothes were flecked with white. She might have expected them to move closer to the fire to warm themselves, but they had eyes for her alone.

"Well done," Malena said to Beth. She walked forward with a vial in each hand. "Tell them to drink this. They will fall into a slumber and be aware of nothing else."

Beth handed a vial to each man. She didn't need to say a word to either of them. She willed them to drink, and so they did. As they swayed on their legs, she and the sisters caught them and lowered them to the ground. Their eyes closed and they lay there, peaceful and still as firelight flickered across their faces.

"It's time, Scarlett," Malena said. "You go first. Then we will perform our ritual."

Beth knelt beside the skinnier man. Doubt nudged at the back of her mind, reminding her that it wasn't too late. She'd done nothing wrong yet. But that doubt was stamped down by the part of her that *wanted* to do this, that hungered for the life force she could sense. She removed her gloves and gave them to

Tilda. Then she placed a hand on either side of the old man's face.

It was instant, the flood of energy that streamed from his body into hers. The man twitched in his sleep, as though a subconscious part of his body fought back, but Beth never lost contact with his skin. She felt his pulse weakening and his shudders subsiding, and as the energy resonating through her body intensified to a brilliant, warm glow, the man finally stilled.

"It is done," Malena said. "His heart beats no more."

Beth breathed out slowly and pulled her hands back.

I killed someone.

She let the knowledge settle into her being, waiting to feel horrified, sickened, but all feeling was eclipsed by the brilliant rush of power flooding her veins. This wasn't death. Not even close. This was *life* and it was hers—every glorious drop of it.

CHAPTER FIFTEEN

SCARLETT STRODE ALONG THE TUNNELS TOWARD HER BED-room, aglow with the vibrancy of life still rippling through her body. After demonstrating their own ritual—a process involving an ancient knife and foreign, guttural words—Malena and Sorena had taught Scarlett how to pour the man's energy into an orb for later use. It left her hands as a stream of gold. Almost liquid, almost smoke, but somehow neither. There had been so much of it, and the excess lingered in her veins, lightening her steps and tinting the world with warmth.

She was nearing her door when footsteps coming toward her made her look up. "Oh, hi," Thoren said. "How did it go tonight?"

That jolt—the same jolt she used to feel when she first noticed Jack as someone more than just the brother of her best friend—pulsed through her. She could lie to herself as much as she wished, but in the back of her mind, she knew she was attracted to Thoren. His easygoing nature, his patience whenever she encountered something new, his sense of humor. And those eyes ... They captivated her in the same way her own siren power captivated others.

"It went well," she said, smiling and clasping her hands together behind her back. "I'm glad your mother and the others pushed me to do it."

"So you were okay with it? With ending someone's life?"

"I ..." Her guilt was an invisible layer buried so far beneath the warm glow that she could barely feel it. "I was. I think all I can really say is that ... I was born for this. I see that now." She leaned against her door, her fingers playing absently with the edge of her cloak. "A mountain lion shouldn't feel bad for killing a deer. The mountain lion was made to do that. And maybe I, in the same way, am made to do this."

Thoren's eyes crinkled at the edges. "I couldn't agree with you more. Tilda must be so happy. She told me last night after you went to bed how scared she was that you might want to leave. I think you've ended up being the closest friend she's ever had, and she was so worried you'd never understand about using human energy."

Closest friend ...

Scarlett's smile dimmed as she remembered Zoe. Zoe was supposed to be her closest friend. And yet ... everything from Scarlett's old life seemed so dull, so trivial in comparison with the immense power she'd discovered tonight. Zoe, a human, could never possibly understand that.

"So you're definitely going to go through with the Change?" Thoren asked. "Become a witch?"

She blinked away the disconcerting thoughts of Zoe and said, "I am."

He nodded, then swallowed and looked away. "Remember when I told you that I don't want to stay here? That I want to travel and see the world? Well ..." He rubbed one hand across the back of his neck, then forced a laugh out. "It feels so awkward to say this out loud. I—I think I would want to stay if ... if you were also here."

Scarlett's eyes went instantly to his wrist, but his charm was still there. She frowned and pushed away from the door. "Thoren ..."

"Don't worry," he said. "I'm in complete control of what I'm saying." He took a step toward her. "Of what I'm feeling." Another step. "That day in your bedroom, when I almost kissed you while under your influence ... After I put the bracelet back on ... I still wanted that kiss. And it was *me* wanting it. The real me, not the powerless version you could command at will." He stood so close now that she could feel his breath. "Do you ... do you ever feel the same way?" he whispered.

Her heart hammered in her chest. She knew she shouldn't, but she did, she *did* feel the same way. His nearness was intoxicating, like a drug she couldn't remember taking but whose effects were undeniable. She nodded as she reached up with one gloved hand and touched the side of his face. She ran her satin covered thumb over his mouth. His breaths became shallower and his lips parted. And then, without warning, he pulled her to him. She didn't resist. Their lips pressed together, hungry, desperate. His fingers dug into her back while hers raked through his hair. His body lined every inch of hers. Nothing could get between them. Nothing except—

An image of Jack.

Scarlett pushed Thoren away and took a few unsteady steps backward. "I ... I can't ..." But then a thought struck her. "Wait." Her hand rose slowly and touched her lips. "You're fine. I touched you, but you're fine."

He blinked. "Yes. I am."

"Do you think ... maybe ... because I can now control the rest of my magic, I automatically have control over this power too?"

"Maybe. Should ... should we test it again?"

Test it again? Did he mean *kiss* again? She couldn't do that. She wanted to but she couldn't. *Shouldn't.* Not when she still had Jack and her heart beat shame into her with every thump. But they didn't have to kiss in order to test this. "Okay," she said, slowly removing one glove. She stepped closer and held her hand out to him.

Tentatively, Thoren took it, his eyes locked on hers. There was a single moment in which hope rose between them, tangible and warm and wonderful—before Thoren's eyes widened in fear and his next breath came in a gasp. He ripped his hand from hers and clutched his chest. He tried to brace himself against the wall and ended up sliding against it to the floor.

"No, no, no." Scarlett tugged her glove back on before dropping to Thoren's side. Tears ached behind her eyes. "I didn't mean to hurt you, I promise."

"It's okay," he gasped. "It's okay, I'm okay."

"This *isn't* okay." She forced the tears back before they could escape. "I hate that I have no control over this."

He reached for her hand and squeezed it. "It is okay," he said as his breathing began to even out. "It's better than okay because we just discovered something. Something good."

Scarlett's eyes raked over the strong man she had unintentionally reduced to something so weak. "How is this *good*?"

"Your hands," he said, "are the only part of you that's dangerous. Other types of touch ... a kiss, your lips ... they don't hurt anyone."

A small breathy laugh escaped her as she realized he was right. This was something new, something she hadn't known about herself. And if she had control over other parts of her body, then surely it wouldn't be long before she could control the magic leaving her hands. She slipped her gloved fingers between his. "I'm still sorry, though. Do you feel okay?"

"I've been worse. Just feeling a little weak, that's all."

Scarlett smirked. "I'll bet there's a charm spell to help fix that."

"There is, actually." Thoren moved as if to get to his feet, and Scarlett hooked her hand under his arm to help him up.

"Do you need a new bracelet for that?"

"Yeah, I'll just—"

"You go lie down," Scarlett said. "I'll get it for you."

He raised an eyebrow. "I can still walk, you know."

"Is that why your legs seem to be shuddering beneath your weight?" She laughed and rolled her eyes. "Just go lie down. The workshop's a lot further away than the storeroom you now sleep in." Which she would *not* be staying long in after

119

bringing Thoren the bracelet, she firmly instructed herself.

She hurried along the tunnels, past the kitchen, and into Malena's workshop. The box of leather bracelets was still on the shelf above the desk. She pulled the box down and selected a bracelet for Thoren, one with a piece of dark wood shaped almost like a shoe. She returned the box to its place on the shelf and was about to leave when the enchanted flower in the corner caught her attention. Or, to be more precise, it was the open window of the glass case that she noticed. Wasn't it supposed to be closed?

She approached the pedestal. Perhaps Malena had made some adjustments to the glacier or lava enchantments and forgotten to close the window. Unlikely. Malena wasn't the sort to forget important things like that. Scarlett wondered if she should close the window, but she dismissed the idea quickly. Magic was probably required. Something as important as this flower would surely be protected by more than simple glass. She leaned in to take a closer look and noticed that three of the outer petals were grey instead of clean white. And then—as she watched—a single grey petal detached itself from the flower and dropped onto the cushion upon which the bell jar rested.

Scarlett froze, expecting an earthquake or an explosion of molten rock or, at the very least, a shudder. But there was nothing. Nothing but the sound of—

Voices. Raised, arguing, moving closer to the workshop. Scarlett dropped to her hands and knees and scooted behind the workbench as Tilda and Malena entered the room. They flung words back and forth at each other like punches, and

Scarlett wished she knew what they were saying. Then she heard her name—and she wished with all her heart she'd made the effort to begin learning their language.

But that was unnecessary, she realized suddenly, because she had a charm in her hand and she remembered the words Thoren had uttered. She put the bracelet on and tightened her fist around the wooden charm—then flinched as one of the sisters brought a fist down on the workbench surface, causing all the glassware to rattle. As Tilda shouted over Malena, Scarlett whispered the three words she remembered. She forced a pulse of magic from her hand, then bent over it to shield the resulting flash of light.

"—angry? You're supposed to be *pleased* with the work I've done," Tilda said. "I mean, for the love of fae, she spent her whole life in the human world and tonight she *killed* one of them. Willingly. That's a gigantic step in the right direction."

"I'm angry because you're still lying to her."

Tilda growled in frustration. "Of course I am. That was the plan. If I had told her the truth already, she'd be long gone by now."

The truth? What truth?

"Possibly, but you clearly haven't thought this through, Tilda. If you let her trust you for *too* long before you reveal the truth, she will feel betrayed. She'll be furious, and she'll probably leave anyway."

"I *have* thought everything through," Tilda ground out between her teeth. "Do not interfere."

"I don't have time to interfere!" Malena shouted. "Not when I have to deal with the possibility of our home shattering around us at any moment. But—"

"Oh, don't be so dramatic."

"BUT I most certainly will interfere if I sense you're about to mess this up for us," Malena continued. "Controlling her power is the sole reason Scarlett stayed here in the first place, and if you don't tell her at the right time and in the right way that you *can't* actually help her, this will all blow up in your face."

Can't help—"You *can't help me?*" Scarlett demanded as she shot, unthinkingly, to her feet. "You've been lying since day one?"

Malena started, but her wide black eyes narrowed a second later. "What are you doing hiding in my workshop?"

"What are you doing lying to me?" Scarlett yelled.

Malena pressed her lips tightly together before answering. "How dare you speak to me in that tone?"

"How dare you give me the promise of controlling my power when that's the furthest thing from the truth?" Fury pulsed through Scarlett's veins. "What was the point in keeping me here? So you could force me to suck the life from un-suspecting humans?"

"You *enjoyed* that," Malena snarled, and Scarlett hated her all the more because it was true. "You should be thanking me for pointing you in the right—"

"Malena, stop!" Tilda shouted, pushing past her sister and moving toward Scarlett with her hands raised. "Scar, this is all a misunderstanding. We—"

"No, *you* stop!" Scarlett shouted. "You've only ever wanted me to embrace my power, and now I'm going to show you exactly what that means." She tore both gloves off and advanced on Tilda.

"You wouldn't!" Tilda shrieked, stumbling backward until her back met the wall. "We're like sisters, Scar. You can't do this to me."

"If you were my sister, you wouldn't have LIED!" Scarlett yelled, pouring all her rage into that last word. She flew at Tilda and wrapped her hands around the girl's neck. Power rushed through her hands and up her arms, and she squeezed and squeezed and—

A fierce grip latched onto her arm, yanking her away from Tilda. The younger girl slid to the floor while Scarlett fell against Malena. Sharp nails ripped Scarlett's skin. She cried out as she twisted and flattened her palm against Malena's face. The witch slashed at Scarlett's arm, but she was growing weaker already. Soon she was gasping, then staggering, and Scarlett easily pushed her down onto her knees.

Scarlett stepped back, her gaze whipping around the workshop. She couldn't stay here. She needed a—There it was. Half a black candle, standing in a jar of quills on Malena's desk. Breathless, she lunged for it, knocking over the jar in the process.

She held the candle up, snapped her fingers, and thought of her old home.

CHAPTER SIXTEEN

THE 'HOME' SHE THOUGHT OF WAS JACK AND ZOE'S house—specifically, Jack's bedroom. She must have been focusing on it more intently than any thought she'd ever held in her mind because Jack's bedroom was precisely where she landed. She had hoped to find only him, or perhaps an empty room and a few minutes to catch her thoughts, but they were both there, Jack sitting in front of his ancient hand-me-down computer and Zoe leaning over his shoulder, laughing at whatever he was showing her on the screen.

They both looked up.

"Holy freaking sh—" Zoe backed up, tripped over the lamp cord, and fell onto her backside, pulling the lamp and a glass of water onto the floor with her.

The scene froze.

Then, as if in slow motion, Jack rose from his chair. "Beth?"

Beth. How long had it been since she'd heard that name?

Zoe scrambled to her feet and flattened herself against the far wall. "How did you ... you just ... you just ..."

Appeared out of thin air, is probably what she was going for. Scarlett raised both hands. "I'm sorry. I'm so sorry. I should have come back sooner, but I was trying to—to learn how to ..." Dammit. Where did she even begin?

A war of emotions played across Jack's face. In a voice that spoke of months of confusion, pain and anger, he asked, "What happened?" It twisted her heart to think of how she'd betrayed him, how she'd laughed with and dreamed of and kissed someone else. She opened her mouth, but no answer came out. "What did you do to me?" he asked, his voice so quiet it was barely a whisper. "I don't understand what happened. I felt as though my life was being drained from my body. I blacked out, and when I woke, you had vanished. The police searched, but they came up with nothing."

"The police?" But of course the police had searched for her. She had almost killed someone and then disappeared without a trace. That wasn't something that went unnoticed. Jack extended his hand to the side and Zoe took hold of it, gripping tightly. Almost as if ... as if the two of them were *scared* of her. "Jack, I was as confused as you were, I promise," Scarlett said, "but I can explain now."

"Can you?" His tone was wary. "Everyone kept trying to come up with a sensible explanation for what happened to me, but all I could remember was how unnatural it felt. How ... *super*natural. I told myself that thoughts like that were crazy, but now, seeing you appear here—literally out of nothing—confirms that I wasn't crazy at all."

Scarlett slowly shook her head. "You weren't crazy. It's …" She swallowed, then dared to say the word out loud. "It's magic."

Zoe shook her head vigorously from side to side. "No, no, no, no, no. Don't go there. We just—we just want things to go back to normal, and now you're bringing this craziness right into our—"

"I didn't do this on purpose, Zoe. I had no idea it was going to happen."

"Just … you … you need to go."

"What?" Scarlett had known this would be difficult, but she'd never considered that her friends might want nothing to do with her. She would explain the whole story, they would eventually understand, and then they'd support her. That was the way this was supposed to go. "Please hear me out. Just give me a few minutes to explain everything."

"I don't think that's a good idea," Jack said carefully. "I remember feeling …" His gaze moved to the floor. "When I looked at you, I wasn't in control of myself. I remember thinking I'd do anything you asked. I'd go anywhere, be anything. I would have drowned myself in the lake if you'd told me to. And that …" He shook his head, his eyes still focused on the floor. "That terrifies the hell out of me, Beth."

"I would never ask you to hurt yourself, Jack. I would never, ever exert any kind of control over you."

His only reply was silence, and eventually it was Zoe who responded. "You're not denying it. You're not denying that you could control us if you wanted to."

"Not both of you, just—" *Just Jack*, she'd been about to say, but that definitely wasn't going to help her case in this moment.

"What have you become?" Jack whispered.

She clenched the candle in her closed fist. "Seriously, guys, I'm still me. Zoe? Will you give me a chance? Please?"

"I … I can't." Zoe's fingers tightened around her brother's as she struggled to meet Scarlett's gaze. "You've changed. You look … different. You're too beautiful. People shouldn't be that beautiful. I don't know what you are, but you don't belong here."

"Of course I belong here, Zoe." Scarlett's tone was desperate as she tried to convince herself as much as her best friend. Because if she didn't belong here, then where would she go? The magic of her own world called to her with an irresistible pull, but she would never return to the witches. Never return to those who wanted only to use her. "We've been best friends for years, Zo. I belong here with you and Jack. And I know I've—I've changed, but we can figure things out as we go. We can get things back to normal. We—"

"Jack was in the hospital for three days! What if that happens again? What if you do it to someone else? Gah, I don't even know what 'it' is, and I don't *want* to know!"

"Then you don't have to. I won't tell you anything that makes you feel uncomfortable or—"

"No. We don't want any part of this. You need to leave."

"I don't need to leave!" Scarlett yelled, and a cushion erupted on the bed, sending balls of fluff shooting into the air.

Jack's arms went around Zoe, and she clung tightly to his

side. Their eyes couldn't possibly grow any wider as they watched the puffs of white float down to rest on the bed.

"I'm sorry," Scarlett whispered, trying not to frighten them further. "I'm sorry, I'm sorry. That was an accident. It won't—"

"Please just leave," Jack said, his eyes still fixed on the bed.

It was then that she saw this scene as if from high above. Saw it for what it truly was. The predator on one side of the room, and the weak, cowering prey on the other. She would never dream of hurting them, but they were right to be afraid of her. After all, it had been only hours since she'd killed one of their kind, and the part of her that enjoyed it had far outweighed the part of her that was horrified by her actions—if that part even existed anymore.

She did not belong here.

She could have used the candle, but she didn't want to waste it, nor did she want to further terrify her friends. So without another word, Scarlett walked out of the bedroom, pushing down the hollow sickness in her stomach as the last vestiges of her old life crumbled to pieces in her wake.

Jack and Zoe's parents didn't seem to notice her as she stalked out of the house in her glittering dress and fur-lined cloak, perhaps because she didn't want them to. She walked down the path, onto the sidewalk, and turned into her father's property. She had no plan yet as to where to go next, but perhaps she should gather some of her old things and take them with her. Or perhaps not. Did she really need anything from this dreary old life of hers? She stood on the front porch, ignoring the widening cracks in her heart, and considered her options.

And that's when the front door opened.

Her father stood before her, unsurprised, as if he'd known before he opened the door that it was her he'd find on the doorstep. Scarlett folded her arms over her chest and said, "I would ask if you missed me, but I already know the answer."

He waited in silence, his hands clenching into fists at his sides, before murmuring, "You're as breathtaking as your mother." Given the bitterness of his tone, she doubted it was a compliment. He stepped forward into the light of the bare bulb that hung above the front door, and only then did Scarlett notice how different he looked. How much younger. It was in this same moment that she became aware of a source of magic other than her own. "Surprised to see me as I truly am?" her father asked. "I assume you can see past my glamour, now that your own magic has awoken."

"You ... you're *magical*," she said. "What the hell are you?"

"A faerie. A faerie who wanted a simpler life and no magic. A faerie who was perfectly happy living in this world until he got dumped with you."

"You ... you've been lying to me my entire life."

"Oh, I'm sorry." He pulled his head back. "Are you under the impression that I owe you the truth?"

"You're my *father!*"

"And that's why I was forced to take you in when your mother no longer wanted you. I owe you nothing, Beth. If anything, you're the one who owes me."

She laughed, loudly and without an ounce of humor. "Owe you? *Owe you?* For being a spectacularly awful father? You don't deserve to be called *Dad*. I don't even know why you kept me. You could have passed me on to someone else, just as Evaline did."

His eyes narrowed. "I'm not a monster. I've seen the horrors of the foster care system in this world, and I didn't think a young child deserved that. Besides, if your mother ever came back for you and found I'd handed you off to someone else …"

Scarlett shook her head. "So that's why you kept me. You're afraid of Evaline."

Sparks of light danced around his clenched fists, and a shock stung her skin. The same kind of shock she'd felt on the evening of the red dress when Dad had told her to get out. He leaned closer and growled, "I kept you because nobody else would ever have wanted you, miserable, plain little girl that you were. And after you almost killed your own boyfriend with freakish powers that no human will ever accept, I doubt there's anyone left in this world who will *ever* want you."

Fury and pain blazed simultaneously through Scarlett's body. Her hand flashed forward and gripped her father's neck. He tried to fight her off, but she held on until his legs gave in. She let go. As he clutched his chest and gasped for air, she lit the candle. She held it tight and walked out of her old life for good.

CHAPTER SEVENTEEN

SCARLETT PICTURED STEEP SLOPES AND SNOW-CAPPED mountains, but her thoughts were vague and scattered, and when she arrived at the edge of a forest where the freezing wind whipped at her hair, she had no idea where the witch candle had sent her. She pulled the cloak tighter around her body, squinting through the darkness at the rushing, tumbling river on one side and the dense trees on the other. She closed her eyes and tried to hear nothing but the swish of leaves, the screaming wind, the roar of water. Anything to drown out—

I doubt there's anyone left in this world who will ever want you.

A shuddering sob ripped through her at the memory of her father's words. *Not true, not true, not true,* she told herself as she swiped furiously at the single tear trickling down her cheek.

"I am independent," she uttered in stilted, shivering tones. "I am strong. I am powerful." But the words she wished so desperately to believe were torn away by the wind.

As she stood in the blistering cold, clutching her cloak and the candle, thoughts of the witches' mountain teased and tempted her. The crackling fires, the thick blankets and warm furs, the comfort and safety. She had sworn to herself she'd never return to them, but what if they were her only option now? They had lied to her, but did that really matter if their home was the only place left where she might belong? And perhaps, as Tilda had said, it was all somehow a misunderstanding. They had clothed her and fed her and taught her about magic, so she knew they cared about her, even if they hadn't been entirely honest.

And there was Thoren. He wanted her. If she went back to him now, she could give him her whole heart without having to feel guilty about it. Jack saw her as a monster, but Thoren understood her terrible power. Perhaps he was the one she was meant to be with.

She uncurled her fist and looked down at the candle in her shaking palm. To go back, or not to go back. That was—

A deafening roar pierced the night as something heavy struck her back. She went flying to the ground, losing her grip on the candle. Snarling, ripping fabric, hot, putrid breath on her neck. She rolled over, found gleaming red eyes above her, and threw a hand up. A pulse of light and energy released itself and sent the creature spinning into the air. It landed on the river bank with a grunt and a howl as Scarlett scrambled backward, feeling for the candle. Her fingers wrapped around it as the creature—a hairy wolf-like beast—rose onto its hind legs.

Scarlett climbed to her feet and ran. With the river on one side, she had no choice but to go for the trees. She yanked her dress up as she weaved this way and that. The beast crashed into the forest behind her, and a scream threatened to tear loose from her throat as she imagined its claws ripping into her at any second. Then came a roar and a whining whimper, the cracking splinter of branches, and then—nothing. Scarlett ducked behind a tree and dropped to the ground. She pressed a hand over her mouth as a deathly hush fell across the forest. Slowly—so painfully slowly—she lifted the candle. At the edge of her vision, a dark shape slithered across the leaves.

She snapped her fingers.

The shape pounced.

And her scream tore through the night as white light engulfed her.

* * *

The echo of her scream bounced across the darkened ice cave. She swung around, almost slipping, but found nothing behind her. As her galloping heart gradually slowed its pace, she patted her arms and body. No blood, no wounds. Nothing except the gashes in her cloak. She pressed a hand to her chest and closed her eyes. "I am not afraid," she whispered. "I am independent, strong, powerful. I am not afraid."

She opened her eyes and looked for the circle of light that indicated the entrance to the tunnels. She walked slowly toward it, giving herself time to think. She wanted to present a front of strength, to show the witches she was not to be messed with. But at the same time, she had attacked them and they had every right to be angry. Should she apologize first? Demand answers first? Would they even let her stay after what she'd done to Tilda and Malena?

She stopped at the tunnel entrance and pressed a fist against her forehead. She squeezed her eyes shut. She hated this powerlessness, hated that she was once again at the mercy of other people. But she couldn't face this world on her own. The thought scared her more than she wanted to admit.

She found Malena, Sorena and Tilda huddled around the fireplace in the kitchen, mugs of steaming tea in their hands. It must be late by now, but perhaps this was normal for them. Perhaps they sat here every night, and Scarlett simply didn't know. Sitting there, chattering quietly to each other, they didn't seem as terrifying as the black-eyed, sharp-toothed women she'd woken up to on her first night here. She stood in the doorway and said, "I'm sorry I attacked you."

Sorena's hand rose to her chest in fright, and Tilda jumped to her feet so quickly she sloshed tea out of her mug and down the front of her dress. Malena simply sat back in her chair, eyeing Scarlett with wariness.

"You came back," Tilda said. She left her mug on the table and rushed across the room, but Scarlett took a step back, shaking her head.

"Tell me the truth first. You said I had misunderstood you, but I heard what Malena said. That you lied to me. That you've never been able to help me control my power."

Tilda halted. She clasped her hands together and began picking at her nails. "It's true. I can't help you. But not because it's impossible," she rushed to add. "I can't help you because I don't know how."

"Then why," Scarlett demanded, throwing her hands up, "did you pretend you could?"

"Because I believed I would be able to! I'd never encountered a power I couldn't tame. None of us had. But it turned out that we couldn't find a record of anyone else with this power. Aside from the sirens, of course, but they can all switch their magic on and off. We thought perhaps it wasn't possible after all, but I didn't know how to tell you. I didn't want to break your heart."

"You didn't think that perhaps continually *lying* might end up breaking my heart?"

"Listen, Scar, I'm not finished." Tilda took a step closer. "On the days Thoren helped you with your magic lessons, I wasn't only training for the Change. I was also traveling. I went further north and spoke with witches at various covens, and eventually I found someone."

"Someone who can help me?"

"Someone *like you*." Tilda beamed. "This witch said that she herself possesses this power, the power to draw out life energy by simply touching another being. She told me that after she went through the Change, she felt completely different. She was able to turn the ability on and off at will."

Scarlett narrowed her eyes and looked sidelong at Tilda. "So suddenly my only option is to become a witch?"

"Well ... you had chosen to become one anyway, hadn't you?" Tilda said tentatively.

Scarlett folded her arms over her chest. "Doesn't feel like much of a choice anymore."

"I know." Tilda's voice was quiet. "But I suppose you could still choose not to. No one is forcing the Change on you."

Scarlett watched Tilda, wondering if this was finally the truth. "Can I meet with this other witch? The one who has power like mine?"

Tilda looked over her shoulder at Malena, who nodded. "Yes, we can definitely arrange that," Tilda said, turning back to Scarlett. Her eyes moved down, and she gestured toward Scarlett's wrist. "I, uh, guess that's how you understood what we were shouting about earlier."

Scarlett looked down at the leather charm bracelet. She had to fight the urge to cover it. Had to remind herself that she'd done nothing wrong in creating that charm spell. Hiding in Malena's workshop, however ... Malena had demanded to know why, and the question was there now, barely hidden beneath Tilda's words. "Yes, that's how I understood you," Scarlett said. "And I'm sorry for eavesdropping. I was fetching something for Thoren when I saw the glass window to the bell jar with the flower was open. When I heard you and Malena coming toward the workshop and arguing, I was afraid Malena might think I was the one who opened it, so I hid."

Tilda laughed her gentle laugh. "Silly Scarlett. It was Malena who left the window open. She wouldn't have been angry with you."

Wouldn't she? Malena's grim stare said the complete

opposite, but then the witch sipped her tea and looked toward the fireplace, and Scarlett supposed she might have imagined Malena's glare.

"So is everything all right now," Tilda asked, "or do you have other questions?"

"I—yes, I suppose everything's all right." Malena hadn't kicked her out, so that was good.

"We should get to bed," Tilda said, urging Scarlett toward the door. "It's been such a long day, and before we know it, it will be breakfast time."

Scarlett nodded and turned to go with her, but then she looked back. It was none of her business, but if she was living here now, she had the right to know. "What happened to the flower?"

Malena lowered her mug and looked around at her. "What do you know about it?"

Scarlett swallowed. "Just that it holds the spells that keep your home here intact."

Malena paused before answering. "We thought it might be dying, which would have been catastrophic for us. Fortunately, I managed to heal it while you were gone."

"Oh, that's ... that's good."

"Yes. We wouldn't want the mountain falling to pieces around us as we sleep, now would we."

CHAPTER EIGHTEEN

THOUGH SCARLETT'S EYELIDS WERE HEAVY AND BOTH HER mind and body ached with exhaustion, she couldn't fall asleep. Malena's words played over and over in her head, but it wasn't fear of the mountain falling apart that kept Scarlett awake; it was the underlying threat in Malena's voice. She told herself that Malena would never kill her in her sleep. What would be the point in that? But the thought, the possibility, kept her awake nonetheless.

Sand passed through the hourglass as time slipped by. She had just turned over yet again when she imagined she heard a tap at her door. She stilled, listening carefully. The tap came again, a little louder this time, and definitely not a figment of her imagination. "Yes?" she said as she sat up, hating the quiver in her voice. The door opened slowly. Scarlett's fingers clenched in the sheets as she wished she had a weapon other than her own hands. But the shape that loomed in the doorway was larger than Malena. "Thoren?" Scarlett asked, sitting up a little straighter.

"I'm sorry, I know it's late," he said from the doorway. "But I couldn't sleep and I wanted you to know how happy I am that you came back. So I thought I'd check if—if you might also be awake, but now that I'm here, I realize how inappropriate it—"

"It's okay," she said. "I can't sleep either. And I don't want to be one of those people who cares about what's considered appropriate and what isn't. We should do whatever we want and not be bothered by silly rules."

Thoren chuckled. "Tilda has taught you well. You'll make an excellent witch one day." He stepped inside the room and leaned against the wall. In the dim light of the hourglass, she saw his expression sobering. "I heard what happened earlier after you went to fetch me a charm bracelet. I'm sorry about that. I had no idea Tilda hadn't been telling you the truth."

Scarlett shrugged as if Tilda's lies didn't matter. As if her deception didn't still sting. "We've spoken. It's in the past."

"So you're happy to stay now?"

She nodded. Not completely happy, but this was a better option than attempting to face the fae world on her own.

"And how would you feel if … I also stayed?" he asked carefully.

Tingling warmth heated her insides, and this time there was no guilt to accompany her attraction to Thoren. Sadness, yes, because she'd loved Jack and had hoped to love him for many years to come. But in truth, the months that had passed since she first fled Holtyn had dimmed her feelings for Jack, and the thought of a future without him didn't hurt as much as it might once have. "I would like that," she said to Thoren, tilting her head slightly and smiling at him. Feeling daring, she lifted her blankets and patted the mattress. "What about staying … tonight?"

She could just make out his widening eyes. "You've definitely changed since you first arrived here, Miss Scarlett."

She laughed. "Don't get excited. I don't want to actually *do* anything. I just …" Her smile slipped slightly as the truth rose to her lips. "I don't want to be alone."

He nodded as he moved to close the door. He padded across the room and eased himself into the bed. He pulled the blankets over the two of them. Gently, he pushed a lock of hair behind her ear. "You don't ever have to be alone."

* * *

As if nothing had changed between them, Tilda took Scarlett onto the frozen lake the next day and taught her how to conjure different kinds of flames. A flame that was cool to the touch, a flame she could roll into a ball and throw like a weapon, one so translucent it was almost invisible, and several others. As the afternoon stretched on, their lesson became a snowball fight, which then turned into a fireball fight. Tilda was complaining about the amount of hair Scarlett had singed off the bottom of her braid when Scarlett noticed a figure coming toward them.

"That looks dangerously fun," Thoren called to them.

"I think Scarlett's trying to burn off all my hair," Tilda shouted back.

Thoren's laugh brought a smile to Scarlett's face. She remembered him tucking her body against his last night and wrapping his arm around her. Her face warmed, and she looked down to hide her blush.

"Bad news, Tilda," Thoren said when he reached them. "The High Tester wants to see you now instead of tomorrow. Double-booked or something."

Tilda frowned. "Now?"

"Yes, well, in about twenty minutes."

Her frown deepened. "Fine. Annoying old woman. Keep practicing, Scar. I'll see you later."

As Tilda headed for the cave, Scarlett reached for Thoren's hand and laced her fingers between his. "I think I now know about every kind of flame in existence." She lifted his hand and kissed his callused palm.

"I see." He stepped closer to her. "Do you have a favorite?"

She considered telling him that her favorite kind of fire was the fire he ignited inside her, but that was so corny she almost laughed out loud at the thought. "The one that's almost invisible, I think."

"Do you know," he said as his lips grazed her jaw, "that adding just two words to that spell turns the flame into one that can devour magic?"

She tilted her head back and let him kiss her neck. "I didn't know magic talk could sound so sexy." He put his lips beside her ear and whispered two words. "And when the magic talk is

141

in a foreign language," she added, "it sounds even sexier." She stepped back and raised one hand. She said the words of the translucent fire spell and added the extra two words, but the resulting flame that floated above her hand didn't look any different than before. "How do I know if it's working?" she asked.

"I guess you don't until you try to burn something protected by magic." He shrugged. "It isn't a spell we use often. Real fires are far more useful when living in a frozen world."

"True." She closed her hand and snuffed the flame out. She stepped closer once again and asked, "Will you stay out here and practice magic with me?"

"I wish I could." He kissed her nose. "But I have to do a quick delivery."

"Oh. Where are you going?"

"Uh, somewhere in the non-magic world."

"Not very exciting then." She bit her lip and added, "Can you do me a favor? It's very important."

"Anything."

"Bring me back some chocolate?"

He laughed. "I guess I can do that."

"And then … meet me in my room in an hour?" She gave him a flirtatious smile. "I'll be expecting more than just a kiss on the nose."

She left him choking on his response and walked back to the cave, trying to hold in her laughter as she swayed her hips and hoped he was watching her. Once inside the tunnels, she fetched a towel from her bedroom before heading for the lava room. She would soak in one of the steaming pools while she waited for Thoren to return. Malena and Sorena had gone into the workshop that morning and asked not to be disturbed for the day as they mixed up a complicated brew, so Scarlett knew she wouldn't have to share a pool with either of them.

She rounded the corner and walked down the steps toward the lava room—but stopped short at the sound of voices. Tilda? Wasn't she supposed to be with the High Tester right now? Scarlett leaned closer and heard Malena and Sorena. So all three of them were—

"My goodness," a fourth voice announced. A voice that seemed familiar, but Scarlett couldn't place it. "This room is even steamier than the last time I was here. Don't you get sweaty under all those layers of fur?"

"Don't you know anything about punctuality?" Malena snapped. "We've been waiting."

"I couldn't get away until now," the girl said. "What's the problem?"

Scarlett tiptoed down the last few steps, peeked around the edge of the doorway, and saw—Delphine. Her childhood friend. The siren she'd accidentally hurt before realizing she couldn't turn off her own magic.

"The problem is the last girl you sent us," Malena said. "Scarlett. It isn't going to work out with her."

"Scarlett? I sent you a girl named Bessie—uh, Beth."

"Oh, yes," Tilda said. She was sitting on the stone bench, swinging her legs back and forth. "I found a necklace in her wardrobe with the word 'Beth' hanging from it. She gave us the name Scarlett, though, so we went with that."

A shiver crawled up Scarlett's neck and into her hair. Tilda had been snooping through her things? And Delphine had *sent* her here?

"Anyway," Malena continued. "We thought we should let you know. You seemed upset when we didn't tell you in advance about the last one that didn't work out."

"What's wrong with this one?" Delphine asked. "She has exceptional magic. She's the perfect witch candidate. Why wouldn't it work out?"

"She's too volatile. That exceptional magic you're talking about is highly dangerous. Even if she goes through the Change and joins one of the covens, there's no telling when she might lose her temper and use her magic against another witch."

"Isn't that a problem with any witch?" Delphine asked. "You've all got magic you can use against one another."

"This is … different," Malena said. "I don't like it. And now she's demanding to meet with this imaginary witch who has the same power she has and who learned to control it after the Change."

Delphine frowned. "Imaginary witch?"

Malena breathed out sharply through her nose. "Another fabrication of Tilda's to give Scarlett a reason to go through with the Change. Following through on that lie is going to be more effort than it's worth."

Another fabrication. Of course it was.

"So you're going to get rid of her like you got rid of Georgette?" Delphine asked.

"I still think we should have given Georgette more time," Sorena said. "She was definitely open to the Change."

"She was not," Malena countered. "And, like Scarlett, she knew too much of our ways by then. Scarlett knows even more, thanks to Thoren's big mouth, so we definitely need to get rid of her. I'll admit it's a pity, though. She has such talent."

"Exactly," Delphine said. "You can't waste a talent like hers."

"And I actually like her," Tilda piped up. "It was easy to befriend her—unlike some of the others." She giggled. "Delphine, remember that faerie you sent last year? Celeste? She was an absolute nag. I had the most awful time pretending to be her friend."

"I know," Delphine said with a groan. "Based on what I've heard from the Agdha Coven, she's *still* such a nag."

A bright flash lit the room briefly, and Thoren appeared beside the stone bench. "Oh, look, the recruiter finally showed up." He looked around. "So have you made a decision yet? I don't want to continue the whole boyfriend charade if it's all going to end up a waste of time."

Charade? Ice chilled Scarlett's blood. Had he really said that?

"As if you have anything better to do," Tilda muttered.

"Hey." Thoren lifted his hands and let them fall to his sides with a loud smack. "Give me a role other than manwhore, and I'd be happy to play it."

"Don't be so crude," Malena chided him. "And yes, we've made a decision. We're getting rid of this one."

"Fine." Thoren crossed his arms. "Go ahead and waste our months of work. Waste all the risk I took kissing someone who could have sucked my life away with her very lips. We'll just wait for the next pretty girl Delphine thinks would make good witch material."

"Or *don't* waste your hard work. Give Beth—Scarlett—another few weeks," Delphine urged. "She would be truly magnificent if she went through the Change. Whichever coven ends up getting her would be grateful."

"And you'd receive your recruitment commission, of course," Thoren said.

"As would you and your family," Delphine snapped. "Let's not pretend we're in this for anything more noble than the money."

"I think there is something noble in it," Tilda mused. "We're strengthening the witch population with talented fae." She paused. "And the money's nice too, of course." Another giggle escaped her. Thoren smacked her arm, but he was smiling too, and even Malena looked mildly amused.

And just like that—with aching finality—the cracks in Scarlett's heart split all the way through.

CHAPTER NINETEEN

SCARLETT STRODE INTO MALENA'S WORKSHOP, FEELING oddly calm despite the flames of fury licking at her insides. She looked around, found the satchel Thoren had used for deliveries, and was about to take it when she noticed a different bag hanging above it. A crudely sewn leather backpack. She took that instead; it would be easier to carry.

First, she reached into the box of leather charm bracelets and removed a handful of them. She dumped them into the bag. Then she opened drawers until she found a supply of black candles. She counted ten or so, then added them to the bracelets in the backpack. Passing the desk once more, she swiped whatever seemed useful: a pouch of coins, a blank notebook, a container of chocolate-covered berries, even a small bar of gold. Lastly, she stood in front of the vast collection of spell books. She was tempted to take the biggest one, the one that was often open on the workbench, but it would weigh the bag down too much. She slid two narrower books off the shelf, flipped briefly through them, and dropped them into the bag. And then, for good measure, she chose another two books—one with a map on the cover—and added them to her collection. That should keep her going for a while.

She turned to the door, half expecting—half *hoping*, if she was perfectly honest—to find Malena there, watching her in open-mouthed shock. But the doorway was empty, and Scarlett encountered no one on her way back to her bedroom. She opened the wardrobe and added a few things to the backpack before stashing it out of sight. She surveyed the room with her arms crossed tightly over her chest. It would be so easy to simply walk right out of here and never return.

Far too easy.

She crossed the tunnel and entered Tilda's room. She flung the wardrobe doors open and examined the side where the smoke dresses hung. She wanted a red one. Red was her color. Her name was Scarlett, after all. She picked the one closest to the color of the red dress from that night with Jack. After returning to her room and dressing, she pulled on a pair of black gloves with lace detailing that ended just above her wrists. Then she sat on the bed, crossed one leg over the other, and waited.

And her anger grew like a pot on a stove growing closer and closer to boiling over.

Footsteps sounded outside her bedroom. Her heart thudded faster. The footsteps stopped, a soft knock broke the silence, and she paused to calm her breathing and clear her throat before asking, "Who is it?" She knew it was Thoren, though. Tilda, Scarlett realized as she gave it a few seconds' thought, usually waltzed right in without waiting to be invited.

Her anger increased by another degree.

"It's me," Thoren called.

Scarlett rose from the bed and moved to the door. She pulled it open slowly, making sure her sultriest gaze was in place. "You kept me waiting," she purred.

"I-I'm sorry." He swallowed, and she had to admire his acting skills. He had certainly done—and was still doing—a good job of convincing her that he was smitten. "The delivery took a little longer than I thought it would."

"Of course," she said, picturing him in the lava room. *Charade. Waste of time. We'll just wait for the next pretty girl.* She almost clawed her fingers down his face right then and there, but she managed to control herself. She took his hand, pulled him into the bedroom, and closed the door. She led him to the bed and pushed him down. Straddling his lap, she cradled his face in her gloved hands. "Did you miss me?"

"Of course."

She ran her fingers through his hair. "How badly do you want me?"

He let out a breathless chuckle. "Very." She nibbled his ear, kissed his neck. Her fingers moved to the top button of his shirt and undid it. Fingers, she was pleased to note, that weren't shaking. Perhaps she was just as brilliant an actor as Thoren was. "Are you, uh—" He cleared his throat. "Are you sure you want this?"

"Do you?" she asked in a low, husky voice, sliding the second button undone.

"Yes." His hands spread across her shoulders and raked down her back. She was so disgusted, she almost stopped to shove him away from her. She had thought he might stop her, but clearly that wasn't happening. He would do this. This sacred act that should *mean something*, that would most certainly have meant something to her had she not discovered his lies. How many other girls had fallen for the same charade before going through the Change and being sent off to some coven or other?

But Thoren wasn't the only one playing a role now, and Scarlett had yet to reach the end of her act. So she swallowed her disgust and pulled him closer to her. She wound her arms around his neck and pressed her lips against his. As the kiss became more passionate, she slowly slipped each glove off. She dragged her lips along his jaw and whispered into his ear, "No one else will fall for your charade ever again."

He stilled. "What?"

But by then her hands were around his neck. She dug her fingers into his skin as she squeezed. He clawed at her hands, her arms, but her power was so much stronger than any man's; he'd lost the battle the moment she touched his skin. His struggles became weaker and more useless until eventually he slumped back onto the bed. She moved with him, never letting go. She stared into his eyes and watched as the last glimmer of life left them, as he stilled and his heart thumped its final beat.

She withdrew her hands and sat back, staring down at the person she had just killed.

What have you done? a quiet voice whispered at the back of her mind.

A single thread of control slipped loose, and she yelled, "I know what I've done!" She breathed slowly and deeply, closing her eyes and focusing on the thrilling rush of energy as she crushed that tiny voice into oblivion. She opened her eyes and said softly, "I've given him exactly what he deserves."

She climbed off him and walked to the wardrobe. She changed out of the dress and pulled on pants, several long-sleeved layers, boots, and a thick jacket. She slipped the back-pack straps onto her shoulders and walked out of the room, not giving the body on the bed another glance.

She didn't head for the ice cave. She didn't light a black candle and walk out of the witches' mountain. She walked instead to Malena's workshop. She strode in and went straight to the glass pedestal in the far corner. The little window was closed this time. Scarlett tried the handle, just to see what would happen. As she'd suspected, the window wouldn't open. She could try to smash the glass, but she had a suspicion that wouldn't work either.

She raised her hands and pressed them lightly against the glass. *Thanks to Thoren's big mouth*, Malena had said. Well, thanks to Thoren's big mouth, Scarlett now knew how to start a fire that would devour magic. She muttered the spell and watched the translucent flames lick across the glass case. Perhaps it wouldn't work. Perhaps this wasn't what he meant when he'd said—But no. The glass was beginning to ripple and melt. She stepped back as the entire case slowly disappeared, as if eaten—*devoured*—by the flames.

When it was gone, she moved closer to the bell jar and the flower floating inside. She couldn't only see it, she could *sense* it. Feel the energy pulsing through it, as if it were some kind of being. The fallen petal had been removed, but some of the other petals had a grayish, unhealthy hue to them. Malena had said she'd healed the flower, but that was clearly another lie. One among many. She tried to lift the bell jar off the cushion, but couldn't. Another protective enchantment, no doubt. Pulling her hand back, she decided to leave the jar intact for now.

She lifted both the cushion and bell jar and carried them carefully to the workbench. There wasn't a great deal of space—Scarlett had always found it a messy, overcrowded area—so, with a flick of her pinky finger and a spark of magic, she swept most of the glassware to the floor. It shattered into hundreds of pieces with a splintering and oddly satisfying crash. She placed the cushion and bell jar on the workbench, then dragged the desk chair closer so she could stand on it. She seated herself beside the bell jar, and there she waited, swinging her legs in the same way Tilda did on occasion.

She didn't have to wait long. Perhaps someone had been close enough to hear the crash, or perhaps Malena's magic was connected to the magic protecting the flower and she'd felt the destruction of the glass case. Malena ran into the workshop, followed closely by Tilda. "What the—" She raised both arms immediately, stirring the air into action, but Scarlett laid one hand—one very threatening hand—on the bell jar, and Malena paused her magic. "Explain yourself," she hissed as she lowered her hands.

"I could demand the same thing of you," Scarlett said, "if you hadn't so conveniently explained yourselves already."

"Scarlett," Tilda said carefully as she took a wary step forward. "What are you talking about?"

"Oh, have you forgotten already?" Scarlett asked, frowning in mock confusion. "The lava room. You were discussing whether or not to get rid of me. I'm afraid I missed the end of the discussion, so I'm not sure what decision the four of you came to."

"No one's getting rid of you, Scar." Tilda took another step forward.

"Stop." Scarlett pointed at the fair-haired girl. "Don't move another step."

Tilda took another step. "This is so silly, Scarlett. You're one of us now, so ..."

Her words trailed off as Scarlett pushed her magic outward and onto the bell jar, whispering the words Thoren should never have told her. From the corner of her eye, she saw the glass vanishing as her magical flames consumed it, leaving the enchanted flower exposed. Scarlett fixed her gaze on Tilda and said, "Stop. Moving."

Malena gripped Tilda's arm and didn't let go. "How dare you?" she demanded of Scarlett. "How *dare* you walk in here and touch things that don't belong to you? Do you have any idea what will happen if—"

"Shut up, Malena." Tilda yanked her arm free of her sister's taloned clutch before turning back to Scarlett. "Just think about this. What will you do out there without us? Where will you go? You need our help to—"

"I don't need your help, Tilda. Not for a single thing." Scarlett moved to touch the flower.

"Wait!" Tilda shouted. "Scarlett, wait. Please. I know we haven't been honest with you, but … but we *do* want you to be a witch. We want you to be one of us. *I* want you to be one of us. One of my sisters. It was all a ruse in the beginning. You were just another powerful, talented girl we needed to recruit, but now—"

"But now it's *still* a ruse. Stop lying. Just STOP!"

"This part isn't a lie! We need you to—"

"Now *there's* the truth," Scarlett replied with a harsh laugh. "You need me. And you'll *wish* that you had me, but you never will." Her hand hovered above the petals, almost touching them. "I am independent. I am strong. I am *powerful*." Her fist closed around the flower. "And I do not need you."

"No!" Malena shrieked, launching herself at Scarlett.

Scarlett kicked the chair at Malena, then swung herself around and off the other side of the workbench as she clenched her fist around the flower. It wasn't nearly as delicate as it looked, and it resisted being crushed with a strength that only magic could produce. But Scarlett's magic was stronger, different, and that energy she'd sensed—that pulsing, vibrant energy, more intensely powerful than anything she'd ever felt—flowed through her hand and into her body.

Wind swirled around the room, nearly toppling her over as Tilda tore around the side of the workbench, arms outstretched and rage dancing in her wild eyes. "After everything I've done for you!" she screamed. "You crazy, ungrateful b—"

With a wordless cry, Scarlett gripped the petals in both

hands and tore the entire flower in half. The floor shuddered, cracked, and split, throwing Scarlett one way and Tilda the other. Sand and stones rained down from the crumbling ceiling, their pattering sound mingling with falling apparatus and Malena's wails. Tilda clawed her way across the jagged tear in the ground, reaching for Scarlett with hands tensed like claws. But Scarlett was ready for her. An iron pot was one of the many items that had fallen from the shelves and landed near her feet. As Tilda lunged for her, Scarlett swung the pot at the other girl's head. She crumpled to the floor, her cloud of golden blonde hair concealing her face.

Scarlett dropped the pot, readjusted the backpack on her shoulders, and stood. It was time for her to leave now, before the mountain fell apart completely. She had everything she needed, so—

"What have you DONE?"

Scarlett looked up in time to see Sorena fling a ball of fire straight at her. She dodged, but the fire hit her shoulder and began burning her jacket. She slapped at it with her sleeve, which seemed to help, but Sorena was already around the workbench. The witch threw herself at Scarlett and attacked with her bare hands. The two of them crashed into the shelves. Sorena gripped Scarlett's neck and shook her, squeezing tight and letting out a wordless yell. It was all too easy for Scarlett to reach up and touch the woman's arm. Sorena weakened instantly.

The ground shook. More stones fell from the ceiling. Scarlett pushed Sorena away from her, and the gasping woman stumbled and fell. The flames on her jacket were dead, so that was one less thing to worry about. Among the scattered ingredients, broken apparatus and bits of stone on the floor, Scarlett saw a black candle. She bent and picked it up. As she straightened, silence descended upon the workshop.

Malena's wailing had stopped.

Scarlett spun around, not wanting to be taken by surprise again, but Malena wasn't behind her. Snapping her fingers and still looking all around, Scarlett backed away from Tilda and Sorena. A flame blazed to life above the black candle—and something grabbed Scarlett's ankle and tugged.

She crashed to the floor and felt the candle kicked from her hand. She cried out just as Malena screamed, "I will tear you apart!" The witch scrambled out of Scarlett's reach, pulled her arm back, then flung it forward, releasing a shower of razor-edged stones. Scarlett rolled onto her stomach and shielded her face. As the stones struck her back, she pushed her magic outward with as much force as she could muster. Malena's resulting scream and the sound of stones striking other parts of the room told Scarlett she must have done something right. She pushed herself onto her hands and knees and scrambled away from Malena and behind the workbench. As the ground shuddered once more and Malena lunged after her with a cloud of toxic green smoke, she jumped up, hurtled around the bench, and ran from the room.

Boulders and stones littered the tunnels, and cracks zig-zagged across the walls. The mountain shook, and Scarlett shrieked as the ceiling split apart above her, releasing shards of ice. She ducked out of the way. She needed to get the bag off her back so she could find a candle, but with Malena's shouts ringing through the tunnel behind her, she didn't dare stop running.

But there, near the blocked doorway of the kitchen, was a boulder large enough to shield her. She ducked behind it at the last moment, hoping Malena hadn't seen her. She waited, barely breathing, as the witch's running footsteps grew closer—and then she jumped.

They went down together, nails flashing, teeth snapping, and arms hitting. Scarlett grabbed Malena's hair and yanked her head to the side, then pushed her hand against the witch's neck just as those pointed nails slashed across her cheek. Pain ripped through Scarlett's face, but it was too late for Malena. Too late as her life began to drain from her like water from an open faucet. Ice and rock shattered around them, but Scarlett didn't let go. She held on until Malena's chest stopped rising. Until her eyes became glassy and unseeing. Until she was gone for good.

She tugged the backpack off her back and felt inside for a candle. As the mountain heaved again, she fell off Malena, and there was heat—terrible, searing heat—coming from somewhere. She pulled a candle from the bag as she looked up—and saw the river of lava streaming toward her. Her fear almost knocked her down, but she raised the candle and snapped her fingers. Snapped and snapped again, and eventually there was a flame, but the molten rock was almost upon her, and she jumped to her feet and ran as blinding white heat consumed everything.

CHAPTER TWENTY

SCARLETT STOOD AT THE ROCKY EDGE OF THE CLIFF, LOOKing out across the misty forest below. Across the world that was now hers. She had fled through this very forest in terror, but she felt none of that fear now. It might have been the glow of energy pulsing through her body, or the realization of the immense power she possessed. Either way, fear seemed like a silly concept she had wasted unnecessary time on. A person who could do the things she could do needn't be afraid of anything.

She looked down as she uncurled her clenched fist. A silver chain lay on her palm. She touched the letters lightly, one by one, whispering her old name in the depths of her heart. Then she pulled her arm back and threw with all her might. The silver flashed in the morning light as it sailed toward the forest below and disappeared among the trees.

Gone forever.

She turned back to the area behind her. The witch candle had brought her to this cliff late in the afternoon the day before. She'd sat with her back against an outcrop of rocks and lit an enchanted fire around her to keep inquisitive creatures away. Then she'd closed her eyes and rested, waiting for her scratches and burns to heal.

She walked back to those rocks now and sat on her jacket. She pulled her backpack closer and examined the contents again. Food was a priority—she'd finished the chocolate-covered berries after waking this morning—but she needed to decide where to go first. The maps she'd been studying all morning were fascinating, but she didn't think they'd help if she wasn't able to accurately visualize the destination she hoped to get to. Hadn't Thoren told her to think of places she knew when using a witch candle? So that left the various places she had already traveled to. The clearing in Creepy Hollow was an attractive option. So many stores to choose from, and if she ran out of money, she could use her siren influence to convince someone to give her whatever she wanted. Her conscience stirred at the thought, but she beat it back down before it could gain traction. She needed to survive, and if using her power ended up being the only option, she wouldn't hesitate.

First, though, she needed to find water to clean herself with. All her wounds had healed during the night, but the dried blood smeared across her face would no doubt raise unnecessary attention in—

A twig snapped somewhere behind her. She was up in an instant, fishing inside the bag for the knife she'd found in one of the pockets. Her hand wrapped around the handle. She dropped the bag and looked up to face whatever creature was stalking her.

"Good morning," the man said as he emerged from the faerie paths, his hands raised, palms facing her. He stopped and asked, "Is now a good time to talk?"

A man. What good fortune. She smiled, fluttered her eyelashes, and said, "Come a little closer."

He didn't move. "Scarlett, my dear," he said, "please don't be alarmed when I tell you that your persuasiveness will not work on me. I came prepared."

Fear—that crippling, detestable emotion she had hoped never to face again—rippled through her. She pushed it away and gripped the knife tighter. She might be unable to influence this man, but if he came close enough to hurt her, she'd suck the life from him without pause. "Who are you?" she demanded.

"An admirer of your skills. I have come to you with an offer you'll find difficult to refuse."

"I don't care if you're the king of the whole damn world," she said. "I doubt you have anything I want, and I won't be manipulated by anyone ever again."

"Relax. I'm not the king of anything. Yet," he added with a sly smile. He lowered his hands. "I'm going to be upfront with you, Miss Scarlett, since you've obviously had your fill of lies and deception." He walked slowly toward her. "I'm on a quest to find power. Power like you've never imagined. I was wondering if you might want to work with me in achieving that goal."

She narrowed her eyes. "What's the catch?"

"Catch? There is no catch. Well, unless you count having the opportunity to use your unique magic, as well as any witch spells you may have learned, a catch."

"So you'd like to use me for my power. Like I said, Mr. Not-The-King-Of-Anything, I'm in no mood to be manipulated."

"Scarlett. A mutually beneficial relationship is not manipulation. If we're both upfront about what we want from each other, there need never be any confusion, unpleasant surprises, or hurt feelings."

Her eyebrows drew closer together. It sounded suspiciously as though this man knew everything she'd been through with the witches. "I see. So tell me then, what benefit do I stand to gain by working with you?"

"Aside from the enormous power we'll unlock at the end of our quest? Well, anything you'd like. For a start, how does living in a palace sound to you?"

Considering she currently had no home, living in a palace sounded wonderful. Too good to be true, probably. "What palace would that be?" she asked.

"The Unseelie one," he replied. "I assume you've heard of it. Your mother visited several times, as did your father. It's where they met, in fact."

Her heart thundered in her chest. "Who are you?"

"I am Prince Marzell." He removed a pair of gloves from his pocket and pulled them on before extending his hand to her. "Call me Zell."

Find out how Scarlett and Zell fit into the main series of Creepy Hollow novels by starting with *The Faerie Guardian*.

www.creepyhollowbooks.com

Rachel Morgan spent a good deal of her childhood living
in a fantasy land of her own making, crafting endless stories of
make-believe and occasionally writing some of them down.
After completing a degree in genetics and discovering
she still wasn't grown-up enough for a 'real' job, she decided
to return to those story worlds still spinning around her
imagination. These days she spends much of her time
immersed in fantasy land once more, writing fiction
for young adults and those young at heart.

Rachel lives in Cape Town with her husband and
three miniature dachshunds. She is the author of the
bestselling Creepy Hollow series and the sweet
contemporary romance Trouble series.

www.rachel-morgan.com

Made in the USA
Coppell, TX
22 April 2020